Stanley Oliver is the pen name of a Christian author of poetry, short stories, and plays. *Breath of God* is his first published novel, which he describes as an uplifting comedy of relationships told through the eyes of Stanley, a Messianic private detective in Belfast, as he carries out his investigation into the disappearance of Steven Ford, in a sharp and witty tone, juxtaposed with several more serious and poignant moments that he thinks create a multi-faceted and captivating story. He is 18, with 85 years of experience and lives in Belfast.

In respect to Adonai, Yeshiua, Rauch Hakodesh

Stanley Oliver

BREATH OF GOD

AUSTIN MACAULEY PUBLISHERS™

LONDON * CAMBRIDGE * NEW YORK * SHARJAH

Copyright © Stanley Oliver 2023

The right of Stanley Oliver to be identified as author of this work has been asserted by the author in accordance with sections 77 and 78 of the Copyright, Designs and Patents Act 1988.

All rights reserved. No part of this publication may be reproduced, stored in a retrieval system, or transmitted in any form or by any means, electronic, mechanical, photocopying, recording, or otherwise, without the prior permission of the publishers.

Any person who commits any unauthorised act in relation to this publication may be liable to criminal prosecution and civil claims for damages.

This is a work of fiction. Names, characters, businesses, places, events, locales, and incidents are either the products of the author's imagination or used in a fictitious manner. Any resemblance to actual persons, living or dead, or actual events is purely coincidental.

A CIP catalogue record for this title is available from the British Library.

ISBN 9781398499553 (Paperback)
ISBN 9781398499560 (ePub e-book)

www.austinmacauley.com

First Published 2023
Austin Macauley Publishers Ltd®
1 Canada Square
Canary Wharf
London
E14 5AA

My grateful thanks for the pathways laid out for me which led to my father, Jack, mother, Mary, my first wife with the Lord, Phyllis, my gracious present wife, Carole, her mother, May, her father, John, my two sons, David and Chris, my daughter-in-law, Inhye, and my grandson Ben.

I also acknowledge the debt I owe to all the believing people of the Church sent to guide me into God's Kingdom; my Sunday school teachers, ministers, and pastors.

Table of Contents

1	14
2	15
3	16
4	17
5	19
6	22
7	25
8	26
9	29
10	32
11	35
12	37
13	40
14	43
15	45
16	48
17	50
18	52
19	54
20	57
21	60

22	63
23	66
24	69
25	72
26	75
27	77
28	79
29	83
30	85
31	88
32	92
33	94
34	95
35	97
36	100
37	102
38	106
39	107
40	110
41	113
42	116
43	119
44	122
45	123
46	126
47	129
48	132

49	135
50	137
51	141
52	144
53	147
54	150
55	152
56	155
57	158
58	161
59	164
60	166
61	169
62	172
63	177
64	181
65	184
66	186
67	189
68	192

Breathe on me breath of God,

Fill me with life anew

That I may love what Thou dost love,

And do what Thou wouldst do.

1

July heat hits me as I come from my messianic meeting house. An elderly woman, leaning against my car, straightens up. I know her from media coverage; Mary Ford.

"I know this is your Sabbath Mr Eigerman," she says, "but consider me a sheep that has fallen into a deep ditch and needs help to get out. You know who I am?"

"I know who you are Mrs Ford."

"Inspector Black said to see you. Told me you came here Saturdays."

"Couldn't wait until tomorrow."

"Tomorrow's Sunday."

"Monday, then."

"Felt the need to come today. You'll be busy Monday."

"I will?"

"Finding my son, Steven."

"If the police can't find Steven, what makes you think I can?"

"Police never tried. I've given up hope that Steven's still alive, but I want to know what happened. I want you to find his remains, and who killed him. I want to see them face to face."

"You want revenge."

"I want them to know I've forgiven them."

"To forgive is good."

"Steven needs a Christian burial. You goin' to help me or not?"

"How'd you get here?"

"Taxi."

"I'll take you home. Get in."

2

We're riding from the east to the west of Belfast.

"Inspector Black said you'd tell me the truth, and be reasonable about payment."

"Best to tell the truth."

"How reasonable?"

"You on benefit?"

"Yes."

"Paid weekly?"

"Yes."

"Got a big jam jar?"

"Got a small one."

"Get a big one, enjoy the jam, put fifty pence a week in it until I find your son."

"Think one jampot'll be enough?"

"Oh ye of little faith. If I'm getting nowhere I'll tell you."

Union Jacks flutter.

"So, where do you live?"

She tells me. I stop in a street of houses built for mill workers when the linen industry was in full swing.

She's about to get out. "Come and share Sabbath Dinner with me."

"Why?"

"You can tell me about Steven."

3

We're sitting in a hotel restaurant. We order, hand back the menus. Mary says:
"About Steven…"
"Let's eat first."
"Are you married?"
"My wife, Ruth, died. We had no children."
"I'm sorry, on both counts."
"You needn't be. Ruth is messianic. For her to die is gain."
"Gain?"
"She's with Messiah. Yeshua. Jesus, to you."
"Ever think of getting married again?"
"Wouldn't be fair. A second wife is always at a disadvantage."
"Doesn't have to be."
"I suppose not."
A waitress puts soup and wheaten bread before us, and departs. I say, "Mary, I'm going to give thanks for Yeshua being with us at this meal."
"We call it Grace."

I say: *"Yeshua, we have faith in you, and we will see your goodness in the land of the living. And so we thank you for your blessing on this meal taken in your presence, and for your guidance as we seek the whereabouts of Steven. In your name and to the glory of Adonai, so be it."*

"Adonai?"
"Yeshua's Father. Adonai is plural, three in one, Father, Son, and Holy Spirit."
We finish our meal, and Mary tells me about Steven, twenty-four years old when abducted.

4

Steven was born in the Maternity Hospital on Wednesday the twelfth day of August 1972. Steven's father, Patrick, held Mary's hand as she delivered him a son, weighing seven pounds ten ounces.

The palms of Steven's hands and the soles of his feet were tinged yellow and he was taken from Mary's arms to be put under a special kind of light so Mary and Patrick went home without Steven, which grieved Mary more than Patrick. Ten days later Mary brought Steven home.

Patrick, a convert from Roman Catholicism, had been totally immersed in a Baptist church.

Steven grew up influenced by Baptist teaching, and by the Presbyterian Shorter Catechism, because Mary had been a Presbyterian when she married.

1978, at the height of the troubles, Steven was left fatherless, and Mary widowed. Did Patrick fall or was he pushed? He'd been working on a building site as a hodsman and had fallen from a high scaffolding and bricks had fallen on top of him accounting for his badly bruised face and body. An open verdict was declared.

Steven was six then. Mary got a job in a High Street café working during the hours when Steven was in school. With that, and benefits, ends met.

Steven left school at fourteen, for a year he worked as a newsboy for the Telegraph then at fifteen started his apprenticeship as a joiner. At twenty he was fully fledged, and the firm kept him on. Mary would have liked to see him take an interest in a girl from her church. He took a girl to the cinema a couple of times, but she wasn't from the church.

Steven got it into his head that his father's death was no accident and he had to find out what really happened to him. He didn't talk too much to Mary about what he was doing but she did learn that he found out there were four other men on that scaffold. He didn't say who they were.

In 1993, Steven was working on a building site in East Belfast. He was fitting top and bottom winders to flights of stairs made in his firm's workshop because, had they been fitted in the workshop, they wouldn't have gone into the houses.

Came a day when he was walking from the site following behind two labourers when a car came into the road in front of them. The two labourers were gunned down.

The car turned, then went back the way it came. The men weren't masked. Steven knew them. He went to where the two labourers lay. They were dead.

He phoned the police and when they arrived he told them how the men had been shot and how the gunmen hadn't worn masks.

"Would you recognise them again?"

"Yes."

"I don't suppose you know who they were?"

"I do."

"You do?"

"They're from the West side where I live. They collect protection money."

"Know their names?"

"Yes."

"Want to let us know?"

" William Blair and John Scott."

He picked them out, in a line-up. When they came to trial and he was a witness against them. People wondered why Steven wanted to do that. Didn't he know they belonged to the Northern Ireland Freedom Fighters?

He was in protective custody before, and through the time of the trial. Steven gave evidence that William Blair was the shooter, John Scott the driver. They were found guilty and sentenced.

After that protective custody was removed.

One dark evening a gang of men burst open the front door, found Steven and his mother in the kitchen, and seized him. When she tried to stop them, they shot Mary in the leg, dragged Steven out to a waiting van. Mary crawled to the door to see him bundled in, and driven off. She never saw him again.

5

I take Mary home, she breaks into tears, so I make tea and stay until I'm sure she's more settled.

Before bedding down, I say aloud,

"Yeshua, my Saviour, you have crossed my path with Mary Ford. Right now I'm tired, I need sleep, then you and I will see what we will do."

It's 8:30 am when I wake and decide to fast this Sunday. I shower, shave, and dress. I take my yarmulke, prayer shawl, and drive downtown to my office. I take off my jacket, loosen my tie, put on my prayer shawl, read the Gospels, in the *B'rit Hadashah,* and talk to Yeshua.

– It seems I'm to find the remains of Mary's son twenty-two-years after he disappeared. I'll need all the help you can give me to find his bones.
– I know, it won't be easy to find the men who took Steven. Mary wants to talk to them. Wants to forgive them.
– Am I happy about what we're going into? I'm not. There'll be dark places I must go, evil I must meet. You didn't want to go into the darkness Adonai wanted you to, but you went anyway out of love for us so that we can stand before Adonai with our sins forgiven.
– So I'll go. You said, "How blessed are the poor in spirit." My spirit, my will, sometimes gets too rich. Let your spirit prevail and your will, be done, so that throughout this quest, it's not me who thinks, feels and acts, but you, through me.
– We need the names of those men who were there when Patrick fell.
– And the girl Steven took to the cinema a couple of times. When did they meet? Did they meet by chance? Was it planned that she should meet him?
– Mary doesn't know her name or where she came from. We'll need to see Steven's room and to go through his things and maybe get a lead about the girl.

– Do you think his father's death and his testifying against Blair and Scott are linked? We need to find out.

My phone vibrates and rings. My ringtone is 'Homecoming' in waltz time. It tells me that my Ima, mother, is probably in the park using her phone.

"Hallo Ima," I say.

"Where are you, Stanley? You're not in your appartment."

"Now you're a detective."

"I'm your mother, I like to know where you are."

"I understood Abba, father, forbids you to contact me?"

"Your father can only forbid a wife, he cannot forbid a mother. Are you well, Stanley? Are you eating as you ought?"

"I am well with good appetite, Ima. In the vertical position, and, fighting off rigor mortis."

"Like that you should joke? Are you using a strong sun screen this weather?"

"Are you using that parasol Abba bought you?"

"Dead, I would not be seen with that in Belfast."

"How's my sister Jo-Jo? Still going to marry the atheist?"

"Joanna wants you at her wedding. Your father's not going if you're there. You should hear him: 'Two children I have, one wants to marry an atheist, and the other's a goy.'"

"I'm not a goy, Ima. I'm a Jew who believes that our Messiah is Yeshua, whose, father is Adonai, the maker of the heavens and the earth."

"When next you see him, don't mention Yeshua."

"Tell me about the man, JoJo's going to marry."

"He's Jewish. His name is Joshua Horowitz. He's comfortable. Will you go to the wedding?"

"If I'm asked."

"You haven't told me where you are."

"In my office."

"Such working. Stanley, you should be a nice Jewish rabbi like your father wanted."

"I'm helping a widow find her son."

"It's good to look after widows and orphans. It's in *Tanakh*."

"Read the *B'rit Hadashah*, the New Covenant, it's in that too."

"Your father found it, and burned it."

"I'll get you a smarter phone with one on it."

"I don't want a phone that's smarter than me."

"There's no phone smarter than you Ima. Love to Jo-Jo."

"This widow's son is missing?"

"His name is Steven, he's missing, dead a long time."

"Mazel tov, Stanley. Be careful of the sun in this weather. And no junk food. I'm told detectives eat a lot of junk food."

"Shalom, Ima."

6

Monday morning. I've been with the Psalms of the *Tanakh*. I'm boiling a duck egg, toasting a slice of sourdough wholemeal bread, making a litre of coffee.

As I eat, I meditate on the words:

But you, Adonai, are a shield for me; you are my glory, you lift my head high. With my voice I call out to Adonai, and he answers me from His holy hill. I lie down and sleep, then wake up again, because Adonai sustains me.

My fast broken, I wash dishes, leave everything clean and neat in the kitchen, then phone Ollie Black. He picks up on the third ring and says:

"Called to thank me for putting gainful employment your way?"

"You were ridding yourself of a persistent widow."

"Persistent she was."

"Another fine mess I've gotten you out of, Ollie."

"Don't tell me: You want my help."

"On a part-time basis."

"Can the widow afford us?"

"She can."

"Concession rates for the elderly."

"Mary wants to forgive the men who killed her son."

"Not easy to do."

"Not if it's done right."

"You ever forgive somebody?"

"Yes."

"A friend?"

"Yes."

"What did he do to you?"

"Won't say."

"Do you still see him?"

"I do."

"Ever cast it up to him?"

"Wouldn't be right to."

"Still think about it?"

"I don't dwell on it."

"Still friends?"

"With reservations."

"Think it'll be like that with the widow?"

"Best, if it is."

"You'll be wantin' my case files on the abduction of Steven Ford."

"How'd you guess?"

"It's anorexic. The paper it's written on is fatter."

"No witnesses other than Mary?"

"Everybody watchin' TV. Nobody stuck their noses out to see. Van was found burned out at the Bog Meadows. Main suspects: NIFF, crooks. Alibis galore, Capone would've been proud of them."

"You got nowhere."

"Got bogged down in the Meadows. No forensics. Slug from Mrs Ford's leg was a .22. No matching gun. The case of the widow's son was put on the back burner, then the gas was turned off."

"Who turned it off?"

"The Chief Constable."

"Desmond Hall."

"The same. Took me off the case. Excuse was, trouble at Drumcree, first with Orangemen, then with Nationalists."

"Anybody since looked into Steven's abduction."

"Priority wise it's the lowest of the low."

"Who's leading the NIFF now?"

"Sammy Payne."

"Was he in charge when Steven's father died?"

"No, Jimmy Maynes was. Think there's connection between the deaths of Steven and his father?"

"Wouldn't rule it out. I'll need to talk with Maynes."

"He's dead. Regime change."

"Sammy Payne?"

"Little Caesar. Carries on like Edward G. Maynes' daughter has sworn vengence and he's gone into hiding."

"Who investigated Patrick Ford's death?"

"Desmond Hall. Inspector, then."

"Find out for me how he handled it?"

"I'll let you know."

"Oh! One last thing. What about the girl? Did you find out who she was?"

"What girl?"

"The girl Mary says Steven took to the cinema a few times."

"Never knew anything about a girl."

7

Belfast is no longer the Belfast of my childhood, boyhood, and youth.

I make my way to where there was once a graceful Edwardian building in place of which now stands a steel and glass carbuncle. I enter to get the Coroner's report on the death of Patrick Ford. I come out two hours later ready for lunch.

I join a queue for a 12 inch Italian herb and cheese sub with Italian BMT, salad works, thousand island dressing, and a fruit shoot, which I eat in the grounds of the City Hall, and mull over the coroner's report.

The coroner recorded an open verdict, the jury confirming Patrick's death was suspicious, but unable to reach any other verdict open to them.

Steven Ford, six months before he testified against Blair and Scott, had read this report.

The names of the four on and around that scaffold at the time Patrick came off it, are, David Nelson, Maurice Ellis, Paul Carley, and John Blair.

I phone Ollie Black. "Ollie, where do I find Sammy Payne?"

8

Sammy Payne lives in a self-constructed fortress on the North Coast of Antrim. I put out the word that I want to speak with him. He probably gave Jimmy Maynes a big sleeping pill and is scared Maynes' daughther wants to give him one.

While I wait, I check on the whereabouts of Nelson, Ellis and Carley and Blair Senior. Ellis and Carley are kicking up daisies in Roselawn Cemetery.

Nelson and Blair Senior are still alive. Nelson has alcoholic Korsakoff's Psychosis and is in a mental health facility on high doses of Parentrovite. This, the essence of my talk with him:

"Had he ever worked on building sites?"

"Why should he work on building sites? He owns building sites all over the country."

"Where does he get his workers?"

"All over the place."

"How many men does he employ on building sites?"

"Thousands. All Prods. Won't have Fenians.

Was Paddy Ford a Fenian?"

"Paddy Who?"

"Paddy Ford, worked on one of your building sites."

"I mind him. He went to Hollywood and made westerns."

"That was John Ford. Paddy Ford worked on the building site in North Belfast with Maurice Ellis, Paul Carley, John Blair, and yourself."

"All of us went to Hollywood and got jobs with Ford. Ford fell off a stagecoach and got killed."

"Was it an accident or was he pushed?"

"He was directin' a fight scene. He was a Fenian. Wasn't liked."

"What did you all do after Ford died?"

"Came home from Hollywood and marched on the Twelfth."

"Who pushed him off the stage?"

"Fred Astaire."

"Do you mean John Blair?"

David Nelson laughed, then asked what room I had in his hotel. He was taken into tea after that.

John Blair lives in a housing estate. He lets me in.

"What do you want?"

"Mr Blair, tell me about the day you and your mates beat up Patrick Ford, tossed him off the scaffold, and threw bricks down on top of him." Direct approach.

He goes to a landline and pushes eight buttons, gets the connection.

"Tommy, I got another one here snoopin' about that Fenian Ford. Get over here with a couple of the boys…I told him nothin'. No, not like last time." Connection broken, he puts the phone down.

"What last time?"

"Listen Mister, you should get offside."

"The last time was when Steven Ford was here. Right?"

"He put my boy in Maghaberry."

"What did you tell him?"

"I'm sayin' nothin'. You better not be here when Tommy comes."

"What's Tommy's other name."

"Never you mind. You can ask him yourself if your still here."

"I'll be here."

"You're an ijit."

"Mr Ford. Look at you. An old man. Your days are numbered. You're going to die. After you die you're going to a life after death which will go on for ever and ever.

"There are two places in which to spend this life after death. There's a place with God, full of light, and a place without God full of darkness."

"Listen, mister. I'm a good Prod, and good Prods go to heaven."

"John, if you die full of unrepented sins, God's going to leave you in a dark place. But if, before you die you confess your sins, and surrender your will to God's Son, you'll be with Him in a place of light."

With that the door bell chimes. John makes a B-line for the door.

"Tommy, come in. He's still here."

Three men come in. Hard expressions, meant to scare.

I say, "Gentlemen, do sit down. You're just the men I've been waiting for."

"What have you been sayin' to him?"

"Tommy, I told him to get offside before you came. That's all."

"True enough," I say. "Let me introduce myself. I'm Stanley Eigerman, private investigator."

"I'm working for the widow of Patrick Ford, the mother of Steven Ford. I'm trying to find what remains of Steven, so that Mrs Ford, Mary, can give him a Christian burial and bring an end to her grieving and suffering.

"I began my search knowing that Steven was kidnapped and taken, never to be seen again. Now that might be because he testified against John's son, and John Scott, and because he began to look into the way his father died. He read the coroner's report, and came here to talk with John, who told him something he shouldn't have, then because he lived in the district where John's son was a bagman for a NIFF protection racket, Steven recognised him when he shot two Catholic men. If he couldn't prove William's father killed his father, he could prove that William had killed the two Catholic men.

"After he testified, he was taken. If you four men know where Steven's remains are, tell me. That's all I want to know."

Tommy sneers. "It's not all you want, you want the men who took him?"

"Mary has forgiven them. If they come to her, she'll tell them so face to face."

"Well we don't know, nothing?" Tommy says.

I get up, "Thanks for listening."

"Hear you don't carry a gun," Tommy says.

"If I did, I might have to shoot somebody."

"So how do you defend yourself."

"If ever any of you need my help, get in touch." I give each, one of my cards. "And John. Don't forget. Darkness or light? You need to find your way soon."

I leave.

9

No word comes through from Sammy Payne so I go see Mary.

"I'm making dinner. Want some?" She's in reasonable spirits.

"If it's no bother."

"It's no bother." As we sit and eat, she says, "How's it goin'?"

"Not so bad," I tell her. "Did Steven have a computer, phone, or diary?"

"No computer, and I didn't come across a diary. I packed away all his belongings. His phone stayed here when they took him."

"The girl Steven took to the cinema a couple of times. Is there anything more you can tell me about her?"

"He never told me her name. You think she's part of Steven being taken?"

"Might be. It's possible she was helping Steven, or she was keeping tabs on him for those not wanting him to find the truth about his father. She could be helpful."

"She might know where Steven is?"

"I wouldn't get my hopes up."

"How're you goin' to find her with nothin' to go on."

"Maybe his phone would help. If you don't mind, I'll have a look at his room before I go. Did Steven have any particular friend or friends?"

"One good friend, Stanley Ross. Started in Rix and McBeath's Joinery Works as apprentices together. Steven and him had dreams of ownin' their own firm. Firm kept them both on after they came out of their time."

"No-one else?"

"Not that I know of. More stew."

"If you can spare it. This is good stew."

"I make a pot full. There's plenty. Does a couple of days. Another soda farl?"

"Maybe a half, thanks. Bake it yourself?"

"I did."

I'm eating my second helping, when I get 'Homecoming'.

"Hallo Ima. I'm working." I put it on speaker.

"My son is working, he says. He hasn't time to talk to his Ima who has come out and is using this new phone he sent with the *B'rit Hadashah* on it so that his father, good Jew though he is, won't know that his wife is doing her best to understand why her son, has taken to follow a man who died 2000 years ago."

"Ima, enough already. I only said I'm working. I didn't say I wouldn't take the time to talk with you."

"What are you doing?"

"Eating pork stew."

"Oy vey, I won't let your father know."

"Make no difference, he already thinks I'm a schlemiel."

"No son of mine is a schlemiel. It would make a difference to me. What I'd have to listen to for the next week, maybe forever!" Better he should not know. "Where are you eating this unmentionable stew, and with whom?"

"I'm with Mary, her stew is good."

"This Mary is young?"

I gesture to Mary, she says:

"I'm eighty-two Mrs Eigerman, and Stanley is very helpful. He's going to find my son."

"Not only is he charging you for his services, but you are feeding him as well."

"Stanley bought me a dinner in a hotel…"

"Oy-oy-oy! I should have a son like that. What did you give him with that unmentionable stew?"

"Soda bread."

"Of your own baking?"

"Yes."

"I must have this recipe. What flour do you…"

"Ima, did you phone about anything in particular?"

"Why interrupt your Ima when she is about to get useful information?"

"What was it you phoned about, Ima?"

"It's your Poppa, he's giving me a hard time over your sister's wedding. Not only does he not want to go if you're going, but now he does not want her to marry this atheist, even if he is a Jewish atheist."

"What does this Jewish atheist do for a living?"

"For a living he is a doctor who hates the sight of blood."

"Ah-ha, a Psychiatrist."

"A Freudnik. He's been arguing with your father on the basis of some book called *Moses and Monotheism*. He tells your father that Moses was not a Jew, he was an Egyptian. What I've got to listen to after that! Put Mary on again."

"Mary is on."

"Mary, I'm Esther. Would it be out of the question if we were to meet somewhere for coffee and exchange recipes? Have you ever baked bagels?"

"No, Esther, but certainly we can meet. Stanley will give you my number, and give me yours. We can arrange a date."

"Good, good. Keep Stanley away from junk food in the meantime. Good bye Mary, it's nice to talk."

"Ima…" Ima disconnects.

"I look forward to meeting your mother."

"No doubt she is looking forward to meeting you, she needs a break from my father."

"Have you trouble with your father?"

"Abba has trouble with Yeshua of Nazareth."

"Why?"

"Because I believe in Yeshua, Adonai's chosen one."

"Then you're a Christian."

"Those who are Gentiles and believe that Jesus is God's Messiah are Messianic Gentiles. I'm a Jew, therefore a Messianic Jew. Not that it matters. With Adonai there is neither Jew nor Gentile, just believers in Adonai's Son, Yeshua."

10

Still nothing from reclusive Sammy, so I journey south of the city, over Shaw's Bridge, then over Minnoburn bridge to Rix and McBeath Joinnery Works.

When I walk through an open gateway the sound of saws and planers and other woodworking machines comes from one workshop, the sound of hammering from another. To the right is the office. I go in through an open door and knock on another which is closed.

"Come in."

In I go.

"Stanley Eigerman, I phoned earlier."

"Stanley Ross." We shake hands. "What can one Stanley do for another? Have a seat."

"Stanley, you were around when Steven Ford worked here. I'd like you to tell me about him."

"That was years ago. I own the firm now. If Steve was alive he'd be my partner."

"When was the last time you saw Steven?"

"That would be the day Steve was sent to the building site to put the winders on flights of stairs we made here in the workshop. I never saw him after that."

"You were friends."

"Mates, used to go out together regularly. To the pictures, football matches, and dances."

"Did he ever talk about his father?"

"Often. Told me he was sure that his father had been murdered by the other men who were with him the day he died, and he was going to prove it even if it killed him. Seems it did."

"Did he ever tell you what he'd found out?"

"He said he knew the names of the men who were with his father that day. He didn't say who they were."

"He had a girlfriend, ever meet her?"

"Oh yes, We went to dance lessons. That's where Steve met her; and I met my wife. He was smitten with this good lookin' red head, Jean McBride, that was her name. Came from the country. Very serious about her."

"Know what happened to Jean after Steve was taken?"

"We tried to keep in touch, but she didn't answer our calls."

"You have her phone number?"

"I'm sure we do."

"When you were at dancing classes, did the four of you have photographs taken?"

"Come to think of it, we have a photo of the four of us."

"I'd like to see it."

"No problem." Stanley gets up. I follow him. He lives in a rather grand house back of the workshop. He tells me the house belonged to a mill owner, who whiskied himself into poverty.

"Anna, are you in or out?" he shouts as we stand in the hall.

"What has you here at this time of day?" comes a voice.

"I've brought a visitor. Are you goin' to show yourself?"

"Male or female?"

"He's male, so he won't mind what you look like."

"He's not blind, is he?"

"I'll have him in the front room when you think you're ready."

I'm seated when Anna comes in. I get up.

"You've brought a gentleman, I see." She's a woman with the looks of spring not yet vanished. With love, Stanley presents her to me. Tells her I'm a detective, asking about Steve, and Jean McBride.

"Remember that photo we had of the four of us. Do you happen to know where it is?"

"And you a Stanley, too. Imagine! Now, I won't have you sittin' there without a wee cup of tea in your hand. And I suppose you'll want one too."

"With scones, and jam and cream," Stanley says.

"And you on a diet."

"Aye, but only between meals. Do you know where that photo is?"

"I do. I'll get it."

Anna comes back wheeling a trolley laden with scones, butter, jam and whipped cream, I say: "You have the gift of hospitality, it's appreciated."

"And what gift have you, Stanley?"

"Helping, when possible."

"And who will our photo help?"

"Steven Ford's mother. She wants me to find Steven's remains."

"Ach, poor woman. My heart goes out to her. All these years, not knowing."

"You got to know Jean McBride. Tell me about her."

"Lovely girl."

"Just like yourself," says Stanley.

"I don't blame Steve for goin' overboard for her. She told me that what first attracted him was her red hair."

"And green eyes," Stanley says.

"You noticed, did you?"

"I did, I did."

"Was Jean as attracted to Steven as he was to her?"

"I'm sure she was. She said one time 'He's honest and he expects everybody to be honest.' He had this thing about finding out about his father, and because of it we sort of split up after we tried to get him to let it lie, and get on with his own life."

"For a while I kept in touch with Jean, but after he was taken we lost contact. She worked in the Bank Buildings, but when I tried to see her, they told me she'd left. I was awful sorry about that."

"Do you happen to know where she lived in the country?"

"I think somewhere along the Seven Mile Straight but I'm not sure where."

"May I see your photo?"

Anna takes it from an envelope she has on the trolley and hands it to me. I see four young faces standing, looking at the camera. Three smiling, and one serious-faced; Steven. I recognise Stanley and Anna. The other girl, Jean, has an arm around Steven's shoulders and he an arm about her waist.

They allow me to photograph it to my phone.

Anna asks, "Do you really think you'll find Steven's remains? There's so many that'll never be found."

"With God's help and guidance, I hope so."

Stanley gives me Jean's phone number. I give him my card and come away with the feeling that these good people think I'm going to fail.

11

I go home, make a meal, thank Adonai for it, then for the rest of the evening I quiet my mind to hear what Adonai Yeshua, and *ruach Hakodesh* will say to me.

The wicked strut about everywhere when vileness is held in general esteem. They have caught their own feet in the net they hid, and are ensnared in the work of their own hands. All my enemies will be confounded, they will turn back and be put to shame.

I sleep without dreams, and awaken to be reminded of the words given me last night in silence.

I'm in my office, looking through the contact numbers on Steve's phone, and find a number same as the Ross' gave to me for Jean McBride. Ollie arrives and sits in my client-chair.

"Find something, Ollie?"

"Desmond Hall. Had me in his office, gave me whigs for prying into Patrick Ford's death.

"D.H: Patrick Ford's death was an accident. Case closed.

Moi: His son thought his father was murdered, and then he was made to disappear.

"D.H: His son was taken because he testified against Blair and Scott.

Moi. The death of Patrick Ford was never fully investigated. There was no follow up investigation when the coroner returned an open verdict.

"D.H: Take this no further, Black.

Moi: Is that an order?

"D.H: Treat it as such if you know what is good for you.

Moi: Why threaten me? Truth is what's good for me.

"D.H: Black! leave this alone."

"That's something, Ollie," I say.

"Not only that, the file's gone Awol."

"There's more to Patrick's death than meets the eye."

"Seems so. How far have you got?"

I relate my activities and tell him I'm waiting for Sammy Payne to get in touch.

"He will or he won't, if he does, be careful, Payne's wicked. Colder than liquid nitrogen, and as lethal."

"I have no illusions."

"And no gun."

"I only want to talk with him."

"There's good and evil in this world, and Payne's an evil who carries a gun. You don't."

"I prefer to rely on Adonai, to do the work required."

"You'd be better off with backup, Stanley."

"Thanks for the offer, but no."

"Well, you've been warned."

"What do you intend to do now you've been warned off?"

"Find out what our Chief Constable doesn't want revealed."

"He'll love you for that."

"What's that Yiddish word for unmitigated gall?"

"Chutzpah." I pronounce it Khoots-pah.

"We'll both need it."

12

Ollie leaves the door open when he goes.

Steven's phone is charging. With it, I want to ring Jean McBride's number on the off-chance that she may have kept her old number and contacts.

A large man comes through the door. He hasn't a gun in his hand, but I have no doubts about why he's here, and on whose behalf.

"You, Eigerman?"

"Me Eigerman, who you?"

"I come ta bring ya."

"Well, Icometabringya, to which tribe do you belong?"

"What're ya talkin' about?"

"Tell me I'm wrong; big chief Pain in the neck wants to smoke pipe of peace with me."

"I come ta bring ya, ya comin' or not?"

"I come in peace." He frisks me and finds I'm not armed.

"My car?"

"Unless ya wanna walk back."

First thing he does is look in the glove compartment.

"You're supposed to have a gun in there."

"Not me."

"You got a gun anywhere else in this car?"

"Would you believe me if I said, 'no'?"

"I'm gonna search."

"Got a search warrant from Sammy?"

"You want a belt in the melt?"

"Sorry. I shouldn't do that to you."

He searches the car, finds nothing dangerous. I get in; he gets in the passenger seat.

"Where to?"

"The boss said you'd know."

"Right, Coast Road?"

"Just drive." It isn't until we pass the power station he breaks silence.

"You didn't show me no respect with them smart remarks. I get no respect from nobody. They make smart remarks like you, and treat me like a go-for. They said go for you and bring you back. That's why I said, I come ta bring ya."

"Forgive me, you're right, I did not treat you with respect. I'm Stanley by the way."

He says nothing until we pass through Larne, on the coast road.

"You're not like the others."

"What others?"

"The others, you know, Marlowe, Hammer, Archer, Spenser. I read about them all."

"You're right, I'm real, they're not. They're paper-men created by people. You and I are real people created by God in His own image. You've read about those characters. Which one do you like best?"

"Mike Hammer."

"Why?"

"He don't take prisoners, and the dames all fall for him. He treats them rough."

"And he drinks a lot of rye whiskey, and keeps his hat on."

"But he's got a .45 and big fists and he's respected even though he's hated."

"Know anybody in real life like that? Your boss, maybe?"

"Sammy? He drinks, maybe not as much as Mike. He don't have a hat and dames hate him. But he's got a Glock he took off a dead copper. Gives him respect."

"That's respect through fear. Are you afraid of him…, ah…What is your name?"

"Paul."

"Good name. Man called Paul brought the Gospel of God to the Gentiles."

"Who's the Gentiles?"

"Every man, woman and child of God's creation who isn't Jewish."

"You sayin' I'm a Gentile? I thought I was a Prod."

"You're both. A Gentile Prod."

"What about Fenians?"

"Catholics are Gentiles too."

"What kind of a Gentile are you?"

"I'm not a Gentile. I'm Jewish."

After a while: "Spencer's got a Jewish dame."

"And a dog called Pearl, and a strong-arm man called Hawk."

"Yeah, Hawk."

"You and Hawk are about the same size. Ever see yourself as Hawk?"

"Nobody messes with Hawk."

"You'd like it that nobody messes with you."

"I'd like that."

"You do strong-arm stuff for Sammy?"

"I look after some of his interests."

"Thought you'd have to strong-arm me?"

"Yeah. Like when you were runnin' off at the mouth."

"Well Paul, I have no Hawk to look out for me."

"Which of them detectives do you like?"

"Which? Marlowe, I guess, and Lew Archer. Two knights in tarnished armour. They keep getting hit on the head too often. I tend to avoid getting hit on the head."

Conversation ceases after that.

Coming to Cushendall I say:

"Paul, there's a pub I know where we could get something to eat. My boss won't object to us stopping, would yours?"

"We got time. Who's your boss?"

"A brother of mine named Yeshua. I'll tell you about Him."

13

Paul grew up in the streets of the heel and ankle—Shankill Road. His mother's name was Jessie and his father's name was Jimmy. Jimmy and Jessie are both dead. He hardly remembers them because he was taken into care when they both were killed when a car bomb exploded.

The care home he was put into was later exposed as being a place where no child should be. Obesity and depravity came to the boys, or the boys were taken to the obese and depraved. They were also visited by the thin and sadistic and a boy called Nigel, Paul's friend, died of suffocation. Paul had been brought back alone that night after seeing Nigel die.

Paul felt he had to escape. It wasn't easy but he went out with the laundry and when the people at the laundry discovered him he begged them not to send him back to the home. They phoned the police, and while they were waiting for their arrival he managed to run into the darkened streets of Belfast.

He only knew of one place to go. The heel and ankle, and in the early hours of the morning he knocked on the door of Mr and Mrs Payne who had been neighbours. They brought him in, gave him tea, bread and butter, and when he told them what was happening in the home, they told each other that it would be a sin to send him back, or to place him again in the hands of social services.

So Paul became Sammy Payne's cousin, and those in the street who knew who Paul really was, went along with that story because Sammy's father was well up in the NIFF.

The police came looking for Paul. They searched and questioned, but never found him.

Sammy didn't like his new cousin, and because of that dislike Paul learned to fight, but as Paul grew bigger and stronger, Sammy learned to respect Paul's strength.

They went to school, together to begin with. Sammy was smart and quick on the uptake, but Paul, was slow in his learning, because deep down within him were scenes and experiences which periodically surfaced causing him nightmares from which he awoke, crying out from fear, bathed in sweat.

Paul was removed to a special school. Sammy's mother Lilly walked him there each day and was there again to bring him home. The teachers were good to him, treated him with kindness, and he progressed in reading, writing and arithmetic but not to such an extent that he was able to pass the eleven plus examination. At fifteen, he left school and went to work with Max, Sammy's father, who was a motor mechanic and had his own garage.

Sammy transferred to a grammar school where he experienced middle class snobbery, mostly from one particular boy who humiliated him in front of others.

Sammy told Paul what was going on. Paul said, "Why didn't you thump him?"

Sammy said, "They'll throw me out. But you could thump him for me."

Paul said, "Show him to me." Sammy did, and when the opportunity arose, Paul, masked, gave the boy a beating and a kicking.

Max never involved Paul with the NIFF but with Sammy it was different and, by the time Max died, and Jimmy Maynes was Commander in Chief, Sammy was well up the hierarchy with decided opinions on how the organisation should be run.

Maynes considered him a threat, and decided to kill him. Sammy, believing that you should do to others what they were going to do to you, but do it first, saw Maynes into the Lagan, instead of himself. Sammy took over as Commander in Chief, and brought Paul into the organisation as his bodyguard.

The NIFF diversified from politics into crime with a string of pubs, and a string of brothels. Girls with hopes of a better life arrived in Belfast, knowing no one, and having nothing, except what they had on and brought with them. They were threatened, beaten, and raped. They were put into brothels. They were frightened, shocked, abused; their physical bruises were only a pale indication of their mental and emotional bruising.

It is hard to say whether it was lack of imagination or ill will that made Sammy give Paul the job of protecting these girls from the clients who paid for them.

When first he was taken to see the brothels his heart melted at the sight of a girl called Adelais. She was thin as a rake, blonde, with eyes, big as saucers. She was very young.

"Don't worry," he was told. "We'll fatten her up, and put a special price on her as she's a virgin." Paul told him he wanted no part in what was going on, because the places where the girls were, reminded him of the place he escaped from. Sammy said, *"You're doin' these girls a favour. You're stopping any harm comin' to them. You're their protector."*

"Don't want ta do it. I don't mind bein' a bouncer in the pubs, but not this." Sammy understood the stubborn expression on Paul's face.

"Ach! You're a waste of space! I don't know why I bother with you!"

From then on, Sammy used Paul to fetch and carry and to throw troublemakers out of the pubs, and when he got paranoid enough to build himself a fortress he took him to the North Coast.

14

We leave Cushendall and climb to the crest of a mountain, and begin descending towards Ballycastle.

"Stan?"

"Yes."

"Could I hire you to do something for me?"

"Like what?"

"Like gettin' Adelais out of that whore house."

"Could you not take her out yourself?"

"I said to Sammy to let her go. He laughed, said she was too valuable. I tried walkin' in and taking her out, but they threatened me with a gun. Said Sammy had told them if I tried to take Adelais away, they had his say-so to shoot me."

"What makes you think I could get Adelais out?"

"You're a smart guy."

"I'm not Spenser."

"You be Spenser. I'll be Hawk."

"Paul, I don't think that would work."

"But, will you do it?"

"I'll think about it. Now, I want to ask you a question so be very honest with me."

"What?"

"Do you know where the body of Steven Ford might be?"

"Never heard of Steven Ford."

"OK, Paul, his mother hired me to find his body. She would like to bring him home and bury him."

"I dunno what they do with the bodies."

"Would you like to help me?"

"Get Adelais free?"

"If I need you for that, I'll let you know."

"Ya mean you'll do it?"

"Will you help me find the men who killed Steven Ford?"

"Get Adelais out of there an' I'll help ya."

We don't say anything more until we've driven through Ballycastle. On the way along the coast towards Ballintoy, I say, "Paul, what brothel is Adelais in?"

He tells me and says, "What do I have to pay you?"

"Don't want your money, Paul. Pay by helping me find Steven."

"You don't want money?"

"Sammy pays you, doesn't he?"

"Yeah."

"He gets his money from protection, from pubs, and from brothels like the one Adelais is in. You want to pay me with his money made from the misery of other people. I won't touch it."

"So I help you an' you get Adelais out?"

"That's about it. What about the other girls, Paul? Doesn't your heart melt for them too?"

"I don't worry about the others. Just Adelais. How you goin' to know what she looks like? I got no photo."

"Let me think about it."

I take the car down the winding road to Ballintoy harbour and stop.

"Paul put this number on your phone." I swap numbers with him. "I may have to call you. And you get in touch with me if you find out anything about Steven."

"Get her out I'll believe that brother you told me about is really alive."

"So, where's Sammy's place?"

15

Before we come to Bushmills, we follow a road running into low hills. We reach a farm at the top of one of these. Before Sammy bought the farm, it had a great view of the sea.

We're checked into to a large courtyard, and all is surrounded by an eighteen metre high wall.

Sammy's made the farm into Fort Zinderneuf, with the bodies of the dead patrolling it with rifles.

A man comes from the house.

"Hallo Tony," Paul says. Tony ignores him.

To me, "Raise your hands." I do.

"Jimmy Cagney still in cell six?" I say.

"He's got no gun. He's clean," says Paul. Nevertheless, Tony pats me down and makes sure I don't have anything strapped to my ankles.

Finished, he says, "Come on."

We go inside. The place is open planned to repel boarders. We go upstairs where there is a three-sided balcony with rooms leading off. We go into the fourth room and sitting on a throne-like chair is Sammy Payne.

He tells Paul, "You get lost."

Paul says, "He's clean, boss."

"Listen you dumb ox, didn't I tell you to get? Go on, outta here." Paul's head droops, he shuffles out.

"He's not an animal," I say.

He looks me over, says, "You want to see me, Jew boy."

"You know why."

"Yeah, I know why."

"You know what I want."

"Tell me."

"I told Tommy, Tommy told you."

"Yeah, he told me."

"I have no interest in anything other than the whereabouts of Steven Ford's remains. You know what co-ordinates are?"

"I know what co-ordinates are."

"I think you know who killed Steven, so let them tell you where Steven is, work out the co-ordinates, and send them to me."

"Why should I?"

"For the benefit of Mary Ford and for the good of your soul."

"Aye, I'm like that."

"If you've no thought for your soul or of Mary Ford, I'll go." I head for the door. Tony stands in my way.

"Sit him down Tony," Sammy says.

"Sit and listen," Tony says.

We sit in a triangle with Sammy as the apex. He says, "I got a job for you."

"Not interested."

"Become interested and I'll get you those co-ordinates."

"I know a lie when I hear it. You don't intend to give me anything."

Sammy says to Tony, "Here I am, a reasonable man, offerin' him a legitimate job, and he don't want to take it."

"He should take it," Tony says.

"I'm going to say something very truthful to you Samuel Payne," I say.

"Maybe he don't want to hear it," Tony says.

"I don't expect you to thank me, because the more truthful I am, the more you'll dislike what I say."

"You've invited me to visit you in this prison you've made for yourself, and I find you sitting in the condemned cell on death row. With Tony here, as jailer…"

"Hey! Knock it off," Sammy says.

"You're in the condemned cell, Samuel, because you're an evil man, involved in protection, prostitution and the pornography that goes with it, lying, stealing, cheating, exploiting, murdering."

"I said quit it."

"You're in a prison you've made for yourself because Julie Maynes swears she'll kill you, or have you killed. You're away from the centre of your Paramafia, your power is dwindling, and you don't know who to trust.

"Can you trust Tony? The thought must have crossed your mind. Nobody in this prison can be trusted, you're all are as bad as each other, thieves and murderers, and there's no honour among you."

"Another thought you might have is that whoever serves your meals may be waiting to hear that a new leader has arisen in Belfast, and is just waiting for the word to poison your food."

"Hey!" Tony says, "What are you tryin' to do? I serve his meals. He's tryin' to set me up, Boss. You know I'm not like that. I'm loyal. Say somethin' Boss."

Sammy, the silent.

"If you want to free yourself from this prison you're in, you need to turn away from participating in criminal activities and start doing good instead of evil."

"Otherwise you'll go on being afraid, and you'll go on losing power. You got the idea that because I wanted to see you about Steven Ford, it would be a good idea to use me to find Julie Maynes, so you can kill her, get yourself out of prison, and be Boss again."

"You and Tony are no different. Both your souls are as black as the darkness of the Hell you'll be locked up in if you don't quit your criminal activities, and seek a truer redemption than you, or any other man can give you."

"I'm not here to comply with, or condone your evil, by working for you. If you know or find out where Steven's body is, then do the right thing and tell me. I'm going now."

I stand so does Tony.

I say, "By the way, you can tell the men who killed Steven, his mother would like to talk with them, about her forgiveness of them. See me out, Tony."

16

In Bushmills, I eat junk food as detectives do, at a restaurant in Market Square, and think about how *Yeshua* is named.

This I do because I am thinking both of my father on earth and my Father in the dimensions I can't see. I worry about Abba's soul and also my sister's.

Messiah's name has meaning on the basis of what He will do and has done for Adonai. 'Yeshua' is a contraction of 'Y'hoshua' 'Joshua', which means 'Adonai saves'.

My earthly abba never says Yeshua. He distorts it to 'Yeshu', a Hebrew insult, *'Yimach sh'mo v'zikhro'* ('May his name and memory be blotted out'). Abba regards Yeshua as a false prophet, a blasphemer, an idolater whom I worship, wrongly, as God.

Abba uses Adonai, out of respect when speaking and when reading aloud, instead of the four Hebrew letters *yud-heh-vav-heh*, 'YHVH', which are not to be pronounced. Abba sticks to this rule. With respect for Abba I use 'Adonai' for 'YHVH'.

I say to him, "Abba, the meaning of Adonai, is 'my Lords', plural. He just gives me one of his I'm-not-having-that, looks."

So, I sit in this restaurant and pray in the name of Yeshua, that, like Jacob, Abba will be wrestled with, and brought into the truth of Adonai's Kingdom.

I also commit into the hands of Adonai those I left in Fort Zinderneuf on the hillside. I would have them brought into Yeshua's fold and His Father's Kingdom when it becomes a reality upon earth, as it is in the heavenly dimensions.

You were certainly right, Yeshua, when you said that you hadn't come to bring peace but a sword! My faith in you has indeed set me in opposition to Abba and my family.

I will not depart from my family, even though being your talmid means that my love for Abba, or Ima, or for my own life, must not take precedence over my loyalty to You. Everything else must be secondary to your will Adonai.

Being messianic is more than merely knowing facts about you, Yeshua. It is to continue your work of bringing about the will of Adonai on earth so that when You come to make all things like they were in the beginning, there will be faith on earth.

You know, just how hard it is for me to be one of your talmidim when brother Saul tells me that I must focus my thoughts on what is true, noble, righteous, pure, lovable or admirable, on some virtue, or on something praiseworthy, while living in a post-modern, post-truth era, that has weaponised lies, that is ignoble, unrighteous, impure, without love and in which little is admirable and where virtue has been cancelled as an inconvenience, and that which was once considered sin, has become praiseworthy.

Such is the glar you have me work in. I've made enemies of Sammy and Tony. I had to speak against their wrong doing, just as you spoke against wrong doing Pharisees, and if they hadn't hated you for it, I wouldn't be here to bless them, as you say I must, because, like me, they are of your creation, made in your image, and you suffered and died for them as much as for me. When you punish you do not chastise the good you created, but the evil which is committed by human and spiritual powers and principalities.

I'll have to be careful of that evil, yet overcome it with good. I know you're with me in this. I'm not getting on very well am I? I'm no nearer to knowing the whereabouts of Steven. I'm pretty sure that neither Sammy nor Tony is going to help.

"Another top-up?" The waitress is back with the coffee pot.
"I've already had three, might as well have another." I smile at her.

17

On my way back to Belfast on the Coast Road, I have a tail. They're far enough behind for me to pull into an outlook area without being seen. I sit and watch them go past. Four, with Tony driving. Paul isn't with them. I take the number of the car.

I phone Ollie, explain the situation.

"Another right pickle I'll be getting you out of Stanley."

"A real gherkin, Ollie. They might be armed."

"Sit tight until I call you back."

"Who needs Hawk when I have you?"

"Who's Hawk?"

"Joe Pike."

"Who's Joe Pike?"

"Watson."

"Just sit tight, Shylock."

Not so long after, my phone rings, it's not Ollie, it's Jo-Jo.

"Hi Jo-Jo, and how is your day going?"

"You should be here."

"Where is here?"

"At the home you were thrown out of."

"I wasn't thrown out; I left of my own accord. What's the problem?"

"Abba wants some of your blood."

"First in the queue is Dracula."

"Stan!"

"Why would Abba want some of my blood?"

"For a DNA test."

"Why?"

"He can't believe you're his son."

"I hope you told Abba, that's an insult to Ima."

"I told him. He said, 'Insult to Ima, no, not her fault. When that boy was born, all the babies were put together, what was given to Ima, was wrong baby.'"

"Get some blood from Joshua, and label it with my name and have it compared with Abba's. That should satisfy him."

"You're angry."

"Tell Abba to compare his nose to my nose. Then tell him I love him. How are you getting on with your psychiatrist?"

"Fine. You're coming to the wedding?"

"Abba won't be there if I come."

"Abba says he isn't going to come if Joshua's there. I've told Joshua to stop telling him Moses was an Egyptian."

"Think he'll do it?"

"He'd better. He's looking forward to having a long conversation with you."

"Wants to shrink my head? That's OK. I'll give him the third degree. What about Ima?"

"She keeps communing with that new phone you sent her. Also, she thinks that it is about time you had a suitable woman to look after you. You're coming to my wedding?"

"Wouldn't miss it. Yeshua loved weddings. Ima, no doubt, will have someone on hand she thinks suitable for me."

"I'm sure she will."

"Jo-Jo, I love you all."

"Even Abba?"

"Especially Abba."

After Joanna rings off I sit until I get another call, this time, Ollie.

"Your bacon is cured," he says.

"Had they guns?"

"No. Not even knuckledusters."

"What's Tony's other name?"

"Esposito."

"Has he a record?"

"Not a pixel on the data base."

"Anything else?"

"Tell you when you get back."

18

I pass by Tony and his friends in a lay-by, hemmed in by a police car.

I call at my office, pick up Steven's phone, go home, make a pot of fresh ground coffee, to go with my take away, then playing a hunch, using Steven's phone I punch in Jean McBride's number.

I have no great expectations of an answer. On the tenth ring, a female says,

"Whoever you are, you're not Steven."

"Quite right. You are Jean McBride?"

"I am."

"I'm Stanley Eigerman, I'm a private investigator. I'm working for Steven's mother, trying to locate Steven's remains. It was she who gave me Steven's phone, and I took a chance thinking you'd have kept your own number. Would you be willing to meet with me, and talk of Steven?"

"It's been twenty-two years, Mr Eigerman."

"It has, and Mary, his mother still grieves. She needs to give his mortal remains a Christian burial. She needs a finish to grieving."

"Maybe he should be left where he is."

"You loved him?"

"I did."

"You too grieved."

"Not for long, I had more to do."

"Will you meet with me?"

"I'll meet with you."

"If it won't inconvenience you and your husband, I'll come tomorrow to where you live."

"I never married."

She gives me the address of her farm and directions how to get there. I thank her, ask, "Why did you keep Steven's phone number?"

"I'm not sentimental, Mr Eigerman. I was told that when they took him, they did not take his phone. I thought of ringing his mother."

"You didn't."

"I did not. Sorry, I have to go, cows to milk."

I pour more coffee.

I get a text from Ollie. We're to meet at a graveyard in the grounds of a defunct children's home.

When there, he tells me the graves are those of children who died in that home.

There are names and dates on the markers, one name, among all the others, catches my eye: Nigel Blake.

A bell rings.

"I know this boy's name. How come you're here?"

"When my beloved Chief Constable warned me off looking into Paddy Ford's death, I got curious to know where Paddy was working prior to his death."

"He was working here."

"Yep, Paddy was here on a job. 1978. Number of children died during the time Paddy was here. Shortly after the job was finished, Paddy came off the scaffolding."

"Hall deemed the fall an accident, and didn't investigate further."

"And later I was taken off Steven's abduction."

"Know what I'm thinking?"

"I do."

"Think we can find out?"

"We can try."

"Let's do it, Ollie. We'll start with a boy, now a man, called Paul, who was with Nigel Blake when he died." I tell Ollie about what I know from Paul.

"First, though, there's something we need to do."

19

Ollie and I plan very carefully for tomorrow.

Today, I'm on my way to see Jean McBride; I turn onto the Seven Mile Straight from Clady Corner, and come towards Ballymather. I turn right onto Umgall Road, and proceed until I come to a farm lane on the left. I take that, and arrive at the McBride farm.

I get out of the car and stand before a sturdy 19th century farmhouse.

The hens I scattered when I drove in come back and peck around as hens do. A young man comes from a long cowshed wheeling a barrow full of cow dung. He puts it down and comes over to me.

"Mr Eigerman? We have been expecting you, mother and I. You want to talk about my father."

There is no doubt. This boy is the spit, according to photographs, of Steven Ford.

When I get over my surprise, he says, "I'm Steven, named after my father."

"Pleased to meet you, Steven."

"Mother's in the orchard." He takes me there.

"Mr Eigerman. I see you've met my son. Steven."

Steven goes back to his wheelbarrow.

"Much to my surprise."

Jean McBride still has good looks and a trim figure.

"Now I understand when you said on the phone, you had more to do."

"Come in and let me be hospitable. I would like Steven to join us."

"That's fine." We go into the cool interior of the farmhouse. Into the large kitchen with its heat from an AGA cooker.

"I take it from the cut of your wee hat, you're Jewish."

"I am."

"What can you eat?"

"Anything you like to put before me."

"Now I'm surprised."

"Has the Spirit of God made you a believer in Jesus, Miss McBride?"

"It's not the usual way of putting it, but yes."

"Well Jesus, or Yeshua, as we call Him, is my Lord and Master too. So I can eat anything He lowered in the net."

"You'll need to wash your hands."

"Yes, thank you." She shows me where, and when I come back, says,

"Sit yourself down."

I sit myself down, and she calls Steven, he washes, then, sits down. The food is set on the table and thanksgiving is said.

By the time our meal finishes, we are on first name terms.

"Jean," I say, "on the phone you said maybe Steven's bones should lay where they are."

"I did, Stan. Steve's dead, he's done now with the nastiness of how he was killed. I've told Steven all I know about his father."

"Mary wants to give him a Christian burial. When I find his remains, will you both come to his burial?"

"You're quite sure you will find him?"

"I will, and when I do, I would like you both to be with Mary at his burial."

"If you do, and I doubt you'll succeed, I will come, but I can't answer for Steven."

"I'll come with you, Mother."

"You're thinking, Stan, that I should have brought Mary her grandson, years ago."

"Only wondering why you didn't."

"I wanted to keep him away from all that nastiness and fruitless searching."

"Mary had Steven's phone; you thought she might contact you."

"I'm glad it didn't happen."

I say nothing, just look at her, truly she has green eyes. The red of her hair is un-dyed, with a little salt in it to savour.

"You never shortened your hair," I say.

"Shall we shed light on yesterday's darkness?"

Which is what we did, and afterwards I help her with the dishes.

I drive back to Belfast with a vision of her face in my mind.

Look at you, my love! How beautiful you are! My dove, hiding in holes in the rock, in the secret recesses of the cliff, let me see your face and hear your voice; for your voice is sweet, and your face is lovely.

20

The farm has been in Jean's family since the time when Sir Randal MacDonnell, the Catholic Earl of Antrim, brought her forefathers and other Presbyterians from the Lowlands of Scotland.

Presbyterian McBrides sided with the United Irishmen during the 1798 rebellion and two died; Edward, during the battle of Antrim, and James, by hanging.

After the Act of Union of 1800 Presbyterian McBrides joined the Orange Order which before that date they were not allowed to do. Jean says allowing Presbyterians to join was a ploy by the English ruling class and the Anglican Church, to ensure that in further conflicts Presbyterians would not again side with Catholics. Jean's father, Robert, did not join the Orange Order.

Jean's mother, Jessica, maiden name Hale, had Quaker background, and it was to her that Jean confessed she was pregnant. Her response was, "Well, my girl, you're bringing this child into the world and we will look after it, and take the consequences."

Jean told her mother about Steven who didn't know she was bearing his child.

Yes, they were going to get married. Their attraction to each other was mutual; she was sure they loved one and other, and when they were together they became one in body if not in mind, because more and more of Steven's time was taken up in trying to prove that his father was murdered.

So preoccupied did he become, that communication with him became ever more difficult because all Steve wanted to talk about was trying to prove that one, or all of four men had killed his father.

He wouldn't say who these men were because he did not want her to be involved. He thought they were part of an illegal organisation known to be ruthless, and that she would be in danger if they thought she knew anything about them.

Then came the time when he saw the killing of the two Catholic men and agreed to testify against their killers. She tried her best to dissuade him, but he was stubborn. He would not tell her why he was doing such a senseless thing.

He was given protective custody. She did not see him at all while the trial was taking place. She did not know when protective custody was removed. The first she knew of Steve after the trial was when the television news reported that he had been taken from his home, and that his mother was recovering in hospital from a gunshot wound. She never had the chance to tell him he was to be a father.

After she told her mother about her pregnancy, there was a family meeting.

She had expected her father to be angry, but he was not. He just said it would have been better if she and Steven had waited until after they were married, and it might have been different if she had told him about his child.

Her mother said that was spilt milk, and life is full of missed opportunities for all sorts of reasons due to all sorts of situations.

Brother James worried about what would be said when they went to church; the names they'll put on Jean and the child. Wasn't there something in the Bible to say that no bastard can enter the Kingdom of Heaven?

They agreed they should be peaceable and remind people with love, gently and kindly and with goodness, that since our Lord died on the cross for our sins, even the sins of those born outside wedlock, they too can accept Jesus as their Lord and Saviour and enter God's Kingdom.

Robert telephoned Mr Williams, the minister of the Presbyterian Church and asked if he might address the congregation on the coming Sunday.

That Sunday, Jean had little idea of what her father was going to say, but she remembered it.

"You all know me," he said. "I am the father of two children. James, a son, and Jean, a daughter. Jean has been in a far country, and has returned to me pregnant. I have welcomed her return with open arms, just as I will welcome the birth of her child with open arms. The boy, Steven Ford, whom she loved and was to have married, is one of the disappeared. A brave boy you may have heard of, who testified against two men of the NIFF. He was taken by them, and in all likelihood is no longer alive, which makes the birth of his child, and my daughter's child, one taking place out of wedlock.

"We all know, because Reverent Williams preaches a true Gospel, that when Jesus died upon the cross at Calvary, He put an end to the Old Covenant, as laid *out in the Old Testament, and brought in the New Covenant of Faith, Mercy and Love.*

"Jean is repentant, not of her love for Steven, but for the act which made them one body before they were married. Love will not say that a bastard shall not enter the congregation of the Lord, because Love does not dishonour others; it keeps no record of wrongs. Love rejoices with the truth. It always protects, always trusts, always hopes, and always perseveres.

"I have told you the truth and I am asking you to love Jean and her child, in the way that God, who is love, loves us, you, me, and all who have confessed and repented of our sins, yet are still sinning."

Steven junior was born, and the congregation of the church made no distinction between him and any other baby born in wedlock. Steven was raised by the McBride family. When Robert and Jessica died, James and Jean continued to look after Steven. The farm passed from Robert to James, but when James, working with slurry, was overcome by toxic gases and died, the farm became Jean's.

21

"Something different about you, Stanley," Ollie says when we meet when I return from seeing Jean.

"Can't put my finger on it, but different."

"I've been out in the fresh air, and away from all the dark and mean streets I usually walk in."

"Learn anything from your jaunt in the country?"

"Nothing that would help us pin-point Steven's remains. But we now know that when Steven was abducted Jean was pregnant with his child. Steven never knew he was to be a father. She never told Mary she had a grandson called Steven."

"Come as a surprise to Mary. Why'd she not want Mary to know?"

"Didn't want Ford influence over her son."

"Be in his genes."

"Jean thinks we won't find Steven's remains."

"You of course, told her otherwise."

"I did. And when we find Steven, you'll see Jean and her son at his funeral"

"That's the difference! You like her, don't you?"

"It shows?"

"All in the way you say her name. What if Steven can't be found?"

"Remains to be seen. Listen, have you done what needs to be done for tomorrow?"

"Of course, Stanley. The call at 1900 hours."

***

Before I sleep, I make a phone call.

"Paul, can you speak?"

"I'm on my own."

"Good. Anything for me."

"Haven't heard nothin'."

"Not to worry. Can you get here tomorrow before 6pm?"

"What for?"

"We're going to get Adelais out, and I'll need you to show us who she is."

"I'll be there."

"Come to my office."

"OK."

I fall asleep thinking:

Listen to my cry for help, my king and my God, for I pray to you. Adonai, in the morning you will hear my voice; in the morning I lay my needs before you and wait expectantly. For you are not a God who takes pleasure in wickedness; evil cannot remain with you. Lead me, Adonai, in your righteousness because of those lying in wait for me; make your way straight before me.

***

A new day is with me. I am in my office memorising the street map of the area around where the brothel is situated. There are four church halls.

When Paul arrives, I have a pizza waiting and both coffee and tea.

"I'm here," Paul says.

"I'm glad."

Paul says, "How we goin' to do it? We just gonna walk into there and take her out?"

"We're not going in. They're coming out. By the time we get there, all the girls will all be in a church hall. Eat."

The text from Ollie comes through at seven thirty. It says: *St Arthelais*.

"Paul, let me have your gun."

"We might need it."

"We won't, give." It's a Webley double action revolver. I lock in my safe.

Ten minutes later we get out of the car and walk to St Arthelais parish church which is three streets away from where the brothel is. Ollie is waiting for us, and takes us to the church hall where the girls are sitting wrapped in blankets and being given cups of tea by the minister and parishioners.

"Where are their keepers?" I ask.

"Under lock and key."

"See if Adelais' here," I say to Paul.

He goes searching among the girls and comes to us with a small, frightened girl, certainly underage, wrapped in a blanket.

"Adelais," he says. "What's going to happen to her?"

"She'll be properly looked after," I say.

"I don't want her sent back ta where she came from. Ya got to promise me, Stan; I want her here so I can see she's all right."

"Get her out now," Ollie says.

"Adelais, come with me," Paul holds out his hand. She places hers in his.

We go out when no one's looking.

In the car Paul says, "Stan, tell me this. How'd ya do it?"

"I put a car outside the brothel with a bomb in it, and made a phone call with the right code. That brought the police and bomb squad. The houses and the surrounding streets were evacuated. Their keepers were taken into custody and the girls moved to the church."

"What about the other girls?"

"They'll be in the hands of the authorities."

"Was the bomb real?"

"It looked real, but it wasn't."

Paul says to Adelais, "You all right?"

Adelais makes no reply.

"Maybe she can't speak English."

"Spoke some before."

"Might be fear. Adelais, we're going to a house where you will be safe," I say.

Paul says, "This safe house, can I stay there too?"

"Why?"

"I don't want to go back to Sammy. He don't treat me good. I want to stay near to protect Adelais."

"Adelais will be safe where we're going, Paul. I need your help in another matter."

22

"Hallo, Ima," I say as she opens the door. "I've brought the doctor a patient."

"Oy vey iz meer! Trouble he brings to our door."

"Ima, don't get excited. This child, her name is Adelais. Paul, here, and I have saved from a very bad place. I want her examined by the doctor, my abba."

"This he tells me, and I should not be excited?"

"Believe me we're on the side of the angels."

"Angels, yet. Welcome Paul. Welcome Adelais."

Abba is in the sitting room. The door is open and he calls,

"Who is it, Esther?"

"A young girl is here, more than twelve she cannot be, she needs your help."

"Who has brought her to me?"

"Your son, the detective."

"Send him away. I have no son."

"Abba," I say, "I will go, but you, a good Jew righteous in the law should remember that Adoshem wants you to do what is right and just; rescue the wronged from their oppressors; do nothing wrong or violent to the stranger, orphan or widow."

We go to where Abba is sitting.

"I bring a stranger and an orphan who is in need of a city of refuge. Adonai gave you a calling; from you He expects mercy. Abba, turn your face towards this child and be gracious unto her.

"Tonight we rescued this young girl from a brothel where she was being got ready to be sold to the highest bidders among men who like to violate virgins.

"I bring her here for two reasons, first she needs to be medically examined, and second, she needs this place of safety until I can arrange what is best for her future."

"Doctor," Paul says, "Look at your son, he is a good man. The men who had Adelais are bad. I know, I am one of them, but I am trying to be good. Please, examine little Adelais and tell me they did her no harm."

Abba answers Paul and not, myself.

"I will examine the girl. But it is out of the question that she should stay here."

"Abba," I say, "Adelais was brought into this country to be sold into prostitution and slavery. That brothel we brought her from was her Egypt."

"And who are you? Moses and Aaron?"

"And you, Abba, are you Datan and Aviram?"

"Enough already," Ima says, "Nathan, her safety we will be."

"But Esther…"

"You say you follow Adoshem's Law, then, follow it. Adelais will have room here." Ima puts a protective arm about Adelais's thin shoulders. "You examine, and I will be nurse."

It takes some time because Ima gives Adelais a shower, and after the examination, along with Paul and I, something to eat for which Adelais says,

"Hvala ti." Ima then puts her to bed.

"The child has not been interfered with," Abba says. "Physically she is healthy, but I think there is psychological trauma. She does not speak, even though she understands."

Ima says, "She needs new clothes and toiletries. Tomorrow I get them."

"I'll give you the money."

"I should take your money?"

"Don't take her with you when you get her clothes."

"Your Ima, she has no brains?"

"We must go now," I say.

"My son will be careful?" she kisses me.

"Yes, Ima. Abba, thank you."

"Go. The girl will be safe."

Abba shakes hands with Paul, Ima pecks his cheek, says, "Paul, you look after my son, the detective. See he eats properly."

"Yes, missus. Bye Doctor."

Driving from my father's house I say to Paul,

"You meant it when you said you wanted to be good?"

"I did."

"Don't want to go back to Sammy?"

"No."

"There is something you can do for me."

"What?"

"Tomorrow my friend, Ollie, will bring photographs, and I want you to look at them and see if you know anybody."

"That all?"

"To begin with."

"OK."

"Tonight, you stay with me."

23

I'm frying smoked bacon, sausages, and eggs, with wheaten farls and potato bread. A litre of coffee for me, and a litre of tea for Paul. A great smell lingers as we eat.

"Your brother help out last night?"

"He did."

"Where's He this morning?"

"Right here with us, and with Adelais."

"Thank Him when you see Him."

"Thank Him yourself. You don't have to see Him to thank Him."

"Like I'd be talking ta the Invisible Man?"

"Just like that. You can thank him for this breakfast while you're at it. You know his name."

"Thanks for getting' Adelais outta there, and thanks for this breakfast, Jesus."

"Paul," I say, "I need your help but, I have to bring to your mind memories of when you were in that home."

"Don't like to remember that place."

"Do you remember Paddy Ford who worked there?"

"Aye, Paddy. He was good. Gave us sweeties."

"What was he doing there?"

"Knockin' down part of the house."

"Was that about the time Nigel died?"

"Nigel, my friend. That was bad."

"You told me a bit about Nigel. You were with him when he died?"

Paul closes his eyes and nods.

"Where did Nigel die? In the home?"

"No." Still with shut eyes.

"Where, Paul?"

"Some place with a fat man." With rising agitation. "Fat man killed wee Nigel."

"Know where that was?"

"No. The van that took us had no windows."

"Would you know the fat man again?"

"He's a nightmare."

"But if you saw him, could you point him out?"

"Yes."

"Ollie'll be here soon with those photographs I told you about. It may be he's in one of those."

"I'll tell you if he is."

"Good man. Did you tell Paddy Ford what happened to Nigel?"

"No."

"Tell anybody?"

"Said for the other kids to look out for the fat man."

"Was there any adult in the home that you could have told, about what was happening to you, and Nigel?"

"They all knew. It was after Nigel was killed I got out."

"Good that you did."

"I ended up with, Sammy."

"We'll find you a job and a safe place to live."

"I was thinkin' I could work for you, and maybe stay here. I could be Hawk."

"I was thinking more in the way of a job with motors. Didn't you say you were good with cars?"

"I am."

"Well then, we'll see what we can do, and if I need any help I'll call on you."

As I say this I get up to let Ollie in.

"Hi, Paul," he says, "I smell bacon."

"Detective's nose. Make you a buttie if you like."

"Coffee'll do. Girl all right?"

"Unharmed. Being well looked after."

"Glad to hear it."

"We got to make sure she's not deported."

"We got a start on that," Ollie says.

"How so?"

"We searched the brothel and found a number of passports. Adelais has a genuine Bosnian passport. Her name is Adelais Ademović."

"Stamped on entry?"

"It was."

"Someone brought her in."

"Adenir Ademovic. Found his passport and work permit?"

"Adelais can stay here then?" Paul says.

"More than likely," I say.

"Ollie, got those photographs?"

"Clear the table and I'll show you," Ollie says.

The table cleared, Ollie spreads out photographs and newspaper cuttings.

"Now, Paul," Ollie says, "take a good look at these photos, and point out any people you know from when you were in that home."

There are newspaper photographs taken at the opening of the home, and also at the time when an extension was built. There are also pictures of the staff that were there from the beginning until it closed down.

"That's Henderson; he ran the place when I was there. He liked to hurt us. He lost the head the night the fat man came back with Nigel and me."

"When I tried to tell him what happened, he beat me, and said if I ever mentioned what happened to anybody he'd kill me."

Paul points out others of the staff at the home during his time there. He was looking through the newspaper cuttings when he brings his fist down in a great thump. A cry of anger, mixed with recalled sorrow, brings tears to his eyes.

"That's him! The fat man!"

24

Three days later.

"Now we know," Ollie says. "But how did Patrick get to know?"

Ollie's phone. "Black." He listens, then, "Right."

"Chief Constable wants to see us both in his office, pronto."

"I guess we know why."

"I guess we do. How's Paul doing at the Garden Centre?"

"He loves it and Len is pleased with him."

"Len, the guy you helped a year ago?"

"Chance to show his gratitude."

"Still at your place?"

"He's got a room at the Garden Centre. Services all their vans."

"You moved Adelais. Where is she?"

"With my future brother-in-law."

"The atheist."

"He has her in a very private place."

"What's he chargin'?"

"He's doing it for love."

"Has she spoken yet, other than to say thanks in Bosnian?"

"She has, and I think she has a lot more to say."

"When she does, tell me."

"If it proves germane."

"Nice word, germane."

***

At PSNI headquarters, a visitor's badge is hung around my neck and Ollie leads the way to the Chief Constable's office.

"You took your time getting here," he greets us.

"We thought we'd give you time to reflect upon what you wanted to say to us," I say.

"You keep out of this."

"Then, why am I here in the first place?" Hall ignores this and turns to Ollie.

"You gave me to understand that you'd drop your investigation into Patrick Ford's accident."

"New evidence surfaced," Ollie says.

"Why haven't I received a report concerning this new evidence?"

"Not yet complete. When it is, I'll submit it to the Chief Constable."

"I am the Chief Constable."

"Your replacement."

"What are you talking about?"

"Your cover-ups about the deaths of Patrick and Steven Ford…"

"You should be careful what you say Black, I'll have you suspended for allegations like that."

"Suspending me," says Ollie, "will not make a button of difference to the outcome of this case."

"Persist in what you're doing, you two, and you'll suffer the consequences."

"Consequences being our deaths," I say.

"I didn't say that."

"What you didn't say was that you will go to that bunch of crooks calling themselves the NIFF, and tell them to put an end to us before we expose your father, and how you've been in, and still are in, their pocket, because your father couldn't overcome his predilections which led to him to corrupting children, and killing one whose name was Nigel Blake. That's what you didn't say."

Desmond Hall slumps in his swivel chair behind his big desk. We allow silence. Many minutes later Ollie says, "Patrick Ford, came to you with proof of what was going on in that home and of what your father was doing…"

"This meeting is over."

"Patrick Ford came to see you…"

"I said this meeting is over. Get out! Both of you!"

Ollie says, "We have a full report ready to be sent to the Police and Crime Commissioner."

I say, "It would be better if you would go to the Commissioner and confess the truth. You will have to face the consequences of breaking the laws that are supposed to protect us from our vices."

"Just get out of here."

Walking back to the car, Ollie says, "What do you think he'll do?"

"Hard to say. He may not go to the Commissioner."

"Or he may go to the NIFF."

"Who will put a contract on us. In the meantime, I'm going to see Julie Maynes."

"You know where she is?"

"She contacted me."

"I'll work on that report for the Crime Commissioner."

25

How blessed are those who reject the advice of the wicked, don't stand on the way of sinners or sit where scoffers sit! Their delight is in Adonai's Torah; on his Torah they meditate day and night. They are like trees planted by streams— they bear their fruit in season, their leaves never wither, everything they do, succeeds. Not so the wicked, who are like chaff driven by the wind. For this reason the wicked won't stand up to the judgment, nor will sinners at the gathering of the righteous. For Adonai watches over the way of the righteous, but the way of the wicked is doomed.

I meet Julie Maynes outside the tropical house, Botanic Gardens. I arrive at the appointed time.

"Are we going in?"

"No, we'll walk."

We walk together and reach the rose garden. We walk up and down among the beds.

"Why do you want to see me?"

"You've seen Payne. You've been in that place he has up there. I want to know how to get at him."

"To kill him."

"Will you help me get to him?"

"No, I won't."

"I have records, documents you'd be interested in."

"Your father's."

"Yes."

"They may interest me, but I'm not going to help you kill Samuel Payne. Tell me, Julie, are you happy?"

"What's that got to do with anything?"

"Just wondering. You want to kill Samuel Payne, and he wants to kill you. You're bound to be unhappy."

"I'm happy enough."

"Hatred and hiding, makes you happy?"

"Keeps me goin'."

"I don't think you're very good at hating. Before your father was killed, were you involved in his criminal activities? Extortion, brothels, corruption of children, murders?"

"No, I wasn't part of it."

"You're part of it now. Kill Samuel Payne, you'll be in deeper. You must have planned on a happier life. Let's sit down here."

We sit.

"I was engaged to be married."

"What was your fiancé's name?"

"Adam."

"What did Adam do for a living?"

"He's a neurosurgeon."

"Impressive, and I bet you're a nurse."

"Was. Theatre Sister."

"Equally impressive. And no longer engaged to Adam."

"That's right."

"Still love him, and does he love you?"

"Why are you asking me questions like this?"

"Because I love you."

"You! You don't even know me! And anyway…"

"And anyway, it has nothing to do with sexual feelings or desire. I don't have to know you to love you. Love is an action, and the action I'm taking is to persuade you not to kill Samuel Payne; not to enter a realm of darkness from which you may not return. Adam tried to talk you out of killing Samuel Payne?"

"He did. It's why we broke up."

"Because you wouldn't choose light, instead of darkness?"

"Because I wouldn't choose his way."

"Where were you going to live when you got married?"

"Adam was going to a hospital in Chicago."

"Were you both excited about that?"

"What are you doing with these questions?"

"You never answered; do you love him?"

"I'm answering no more of your questions."

"Then, just let me say this, Julie. You may feel you really intended the words you used when you vowed to kill Samuel; I think later you came to regret them."

We sit in silence, then:

"Why not let Adam know that what he was doing was loving you, and that you've turned away from seeking to kill Samuel. Then the two of you might marry and live usefully in Chicago."

Another silence.

"And if you do, I'll tell you what; Samuel Payne will still be locked up in that prison he's created for himself thinking you are out there in the darkness waiting to kill him, or have him killed.

"I'd rather come to your wedding than attend your funeral." I get up.

"I have to go. Stay in the light, Julie. I hope, in the meantime, you have a safe place to hide from the men Sammy has looking for you. You'll be safer in America."

"You're loving me again."

"I am, and you should love Adam."

26

Phone. This time it's Mary:

"Stan, a man called wanting to see me."

"Did he give a name?"

"John Blair. Said he wanted to tell me something about Paddy. I'd like you to be here when he comes."

"When is he coming?"

"Eight, tonight."

"I'll be there."

***

Mary brings John Blair into her parlour where I'm sitting beside a tray with tea, sandwiches, and biscuits.

"Mr Eigerman is here, you won't mind?" Mary says.

"Well, I…It's kinda awkward."

"Sit down, Mr Blair. What is it you want to tell me?"

"It's about what he said." Nods towards me.

"What did I say?"

"You said Mrs Ford wanted to forgive the men who killed her son."

"I did."

"I want her to forgive me?"

"What have I got to forgive you for, Mr Blair?"

"For killin' your husband, missus."

Mary pours tea; offers sandwiches.

"Why wait all this time before telling me?"

"I had to come now because of somethin' else he said."

"What was that?"

"He said I'd live forever in the dark. I don't like the dark."

"Mr Blair, let me tell you something. When you killed my Paddy, you left me with photographs and mementoes, but photographs and things don't take the place of Paddy's voice, his face, or his hand in mine."

"Ach, missus…yer hurtin' me."

"You hurt me."

"You're not goin' to forgive me, sure you're not? You'd rather I ended up in a dark place."

"I don't want you to end up in a dark place Mr Blair. God help me, I forgive you, murderer of my husband, and thief of the years we should have had together."

"Ach…"

"We'll say nothing more about it. But you'll still be in the dark place if you don't ask God to forgive you."

I say, "Do you know where Mary's son Steven is, for that is another wound in her heart, another sorrow."

"I don't know, honest."

"Leave the poor man alone," Mary says. "Let him go home and get on his knees."

"Will youse be tellin' the polis?"

"Better if you tell them."

"I'll go then?"

"Who gave you orders to kill Paddy?"

"Jimmy Maynes."

"Who gave him his orders?"

"Dunno."

"Go, John, and be careful with your soul."

"You all right?" I ask Mary, after John Blair has gone.

"I wanted to slap his face, to hurt him."

"You probably hurt him more, offering tea and a sandwich, and by what you said."

"Have the rest of these sandwiches. I'll tell your Ima that you're not eating junk food."

"When are you meeting?"

"Day after tomorrow."

27

I begin another day with the Tehillim:

Make me grasp, Adonai, what my end must be, what it means that my days are numbered; let me know what a transient creature I am. You have made my days like handbreadths; for you, the length of my life is like nothing. Yes, everyone, no matter how firmly he stands, is merely a puff of wind. Humans go about like shadows; their turmoil is all for nothing. They accumulate wealth, not knowing who will enjoy its benefits. Now, Adonai, what am I waiting for? You are my only hope…Yes, everyone is merely a puff of wind.

Phone.

"Ollie."

"You watching' the television?"

"What is it?"

"Local news."

I turn on. The Chief Constable came out of his house and was shot by a gunman who fled on a motorcycle. Taken to hospital.

"Been to the hospital," Ollie's says. "He's in surgery, his chances are slim."

"We may be next."

"Best to be on our guard."

"We're all transient creatures."

"'tis so, 'tis so."

"Ollie terminates; I cut off the TV I think of my car in the street.

My garage is full of junk, so I make a clearance and get my car in.

I sit in my car, and think. I'm there when Ollie rings again."

"He didn't make it. What are you doing?"

"Sitting in my car, thinking."

"I'll come join you."

Ollie comes, sits beside me on the passenger seat.

"Motor pool?"

"Yeah. So, what are your thoughts?"

"Think the best, prepare for the worst."

"Great minds."

"Fools seldom differ. He's told them about us."

"Let's think some more on a full stomach," I say.

"Well," says Ollie, after we've eaten. "That wasn't bad for Jewish cookin'"

"Good to see a clean plate."

"What we should be thinking about, Stanley, is what to do if Desmond Hall has put a target on our backs."

"I would like to know, Ollie, who he went to about what we said to him."

"Something we need to find out."

"Business as usual. I still have to find Steven, and you have to maintain law and order."

"You need a gun, licence, and permit."

"I need a gun like a hole in the head."

"A hole in the head is what you'll get if you don't have a gun."

"Ollie, I know you have my best interests at heart but a gun is not in my best interests."

"You really frustrate me, Stanley. What do you think you're going to do? Talk your way out of being shot?"

"Given the opportunity."

"And if not?"

"Probably be shot."

"That doesn't concern you?"

"I'd rather be shot, than shoot another human being."

"That all sounds very moral, but when hardy comes to hardy you might wish you had a gun. Tell me, would you use a gun to defend others, your mother, father, sister?"

"As I won't be having a gun, the question does not arise."

"What would you do?"

"Can't answer, until the situation arises."

"You need to think seriously about your safety, and that of your family."

"I'm not going to build a fortress around me like Sammy Payne."

"Stanley, just be careful."

"You, likewise, Ollie."

28

I ring Joshua, to find out how Adelais is.

"Come and see for yourself," he says. I tell him I'm coming.

I watch for tails. No one is following. I ease off onto the motorway, and head for Joshua's therapeutic establishment.

Joshua is standing at the portico.

"Joshua."

"Come in, I want to talk with you."

"Not about Moses being an Egyptian."

"About your sister, me, and Ifeta Božić."

"Who?"

"The real name of Adelais Ademović."

He took me to where he had his Freudian couch.

"Want to try it?"

"My ego couldn't stand it, and my id may get the better of my super-ego." I sit in one of his two comfortable leather chairs.

"What do you want to tell me about Ifeta, before I see her? Do I need an interpreter?"

"She speaks English. First, I want to talk to you about your sister and me."

"Having second thoughts?"

"No. We're getting married."

"How do you feel about marrying into a family of orthodox Jews, and one Messianic Jew?"

"I can live with that."

"And what if Joanna wants to practice her faith?"

"I'll not stop her."

"Very good of you, but how will you help her to practice her faith?"

"Joanna and I will work that out."

"You'll find it hard."

"In what way?"

"What will you say when she mentions Adonai?"

"Perhaps I shall say nothing."

"Joanna will expect you to say something."

"As you say I may find it hard."

"Because you love her and don't want to harm her."

"Yes."

"Will you ask Joanna to share your faith in Freud, Jung, Adler and all your other human icons?"

"We'll agree to respect each other's point of view."

"A point of view is an external presentation to the world. Differs from an internal belief. Joanna probably thinks she'll change your belief to an acceptance of her belief that Adonai is there, and not silent. Do you think you will change her to accept your belief that there is no God?"

"All this was not what I wanted to say to you."

"I'm sorry. I just can't see how a godless man can have a like-minded relationship with a God believing woman."

"You've made your point. What I wanted to say was this: Joanna and I talked it over and are of one mind about Ifeta, we want to adopt her when we get married."

"Not a wise move."

"She'd get an education and better life chances."

"Would that be a good thing for Ifeta?"

"Of course, it would."

I get up and move towards a framed quotation he has hanging on his wall.

"Does Joanna know about this?"

"She does."

"Does she go along with it?"

"Well, no."

The quotation says:

I DO MY THING AND YOU DO YOU THING
I AM NOT IN THIS WORLD TO LIVE UP TO YOUR EXPECTATIONS
AND YOU ARE NOT IN THIS WORLD TO LIVE UP TO MINE
YOU ARE YOU AND I AM I,
AND IF BY CHANCE WE FIND EACH OTHER IT'S BEAUTIFUL
IF NOT, IT CAN'T BE HELPED.

I re-seat.

"Have you mentioned to Ifeta what you want to do?"

"Of course not."

"If you and Joanna are going to be in conflict throughout your marriage, would it be right to bring Ifeta into the midst of that conflict?"

"Not only that, but Ifeta is about to enter her teenage years. How are you going to cope with teenage angst?

"Are you going to tell her it's your belief that there is no God? Is Joanna going to tell her of her belief that there is a God? And how are you both going to answer her questions? You're going to make her angst all the greater."

"I object to what you're saying."

"I know Joanna, and you think you'll work it out. If you marry there's going to be conflict, until one or the other becomes dominant or there's a divorce."

"Who are you to say this to me?"

"You're my intended brother-in-law and as such, I suspect you will not be able to give my sister the life she deserves, or a teenager the love she needs."

"I resent your whole attitude towards me."

"Forgive me. I did not come here to talk like this. I agree Ifeta needs an education, but she should be involved, when you consider the kind of love she needs. She shouldn't be considered an object to make you feel good about yourselves."

"Let me ask you something, Stanley."

"Go ahead."

"Would you say you are a godly man?"

"I believe in God and His manner of goodness."

"You believe in doing good?"

"Of course."

"You can't be truly good, if you do it to enjoy feeling righteous, and your only motive is to gain eternal life."

"I can say that I know that when I do what Yeshua tells me is good to do, I am aware that I have no righteousness, and I can't say I enjoy any feeling of righteousness. I'm just thankful that any good I do, turns out to be beneficial to someone and yes, I feel glad about that.

"As for being motivated by wanting eternal life, I believe I already have that now through my faith. I believe there is a God and He is already with me, and I shall be with Him when this Earth, which we've corrupted, is redeemed. I don't think of any eternal reward when I do good. I do good in gratitude of what God has done for me. There is always an element of selfishness in everything I do. Nothing or no one is perfect in this world, and I am to some extent the product of my environment, upbringing, and genes.

"You believe in doing good, but you believe there is no God, no eternal life. We can prove who is right, you or I, all we have to do is die."

"I think you'll try to persuade Joanna not to marry me."

"That, I won't do."

"I'll be good to Joanna."

"I know. You'll try. I expect you to love Joanna, by looking out for her welfare more than your own, and if necessary be prepared to die for her. Do that for her, and she will live for you, and give you love and devotion. Tell me about Ifeta, before I speak with her."

29

Ifeta is twelve years of age. Ademović is not the name of her real family, it is Božić, and they belonged to the Bosnian Church which simply call themselves Krstjani 'Christians' or Dobri Bošnjani 'Good Bosnians'. The Christian hierarchies of both Roman Catholic and the Eastern Orthodox considered them heretics and persecuted them ever since they gave sanctuary to Gnostic Cathars in the middle ages.

Even at the age of twelve Ifeta knew this history because her grandfather was a djed, *a bishop of the church, and her father one of the council of twelve.*

During the Bosnian conflict the Dobri Bošnjani gave sanctuary to Serbian Moslems, so that when the Orthodox Christian soldiers and the Catholic Croats overran Moštre, near Visoko where they lived, Ifeta witnessed the massacre of the Dobri Bošnjani including her grandfather, father, mother, and her two brothers.

She wasn't raped and then killed as many other girls of her age were. She only remembers being taken from where her people lay dead, by the man who killed them.

She walked with him many miles. She had no idea in what direction, but they came to a big city, a boarding house, and, an Orthodox Church.

Then more miles of walking, to a place called Foča a town with a river. Days there. The man was always able to feed her and there were streams for water. He talked to her but she has no recollection of what he said. More travelling, bypassing a place called Čajniče and settling down to wait for nightfall, which when it came, she had to be very quiet for this was a border, and there were guards.

Darkness came and they moved. The moon was full and from time to time they had to wait on cloud cover before they moved. One time, the man put his hand over her mouth, then crossing, to a place called Montenegro and to a house where there was a bath, a bed, warm blankets.

And voices: ...image of your daughter, Adenir...feverish poor mite...nightmares she's having...Doctor, is she going...You've got to drink dearie...

For a while, Ifeta had gone to a place from where she did not want to return. She wished to stay in a place where she had no awareness of anything, and where nothing caused her physical or psychological pain.

Ifeta had been silent from the time she had witnessed the deaths of her family, and as her body recovered from the infection, awareness returned, she remained silent.

She was told when she was strong again and able to walk, that she must remember that her name was now Adelais Ademović for that was the name of Adenir's daughter. She must not say her own name. If she speaks at all, she must say that she is his daughter, Adelais.

Then, off again in an open lorry to where aeroplanes come and go. Ifeta carries a small case and Adenir a large duffel bag. Case and duffel are checked in where Adenir gives their names, presents passports. She is looked at, asked her name. She stares at the woman, hears: "She can't speak; dumb," from Adenir. The passports are handed back and boarding passes given.

Searched before departure. Eats before boarding a plane. Fearful at take off, and throughout the flight. Ears popping, and painfull on descent. Bumpy landing in the early hours of the morning.

Ifeta doesn't know where she is. She's in a taxi taking them to a place where they can stay. It is not a nice place, but they're not allowed to leave, and Ifeta witnesses more fighting and the killing of Adenir.

She is seized and taken to another house. The one she was rescued from. Why Adenir came to Belfast, is something we might never know.

30

Ifeta is brought in looking more robust from the last time I saw her.

"Hallo, Ifeta," I say. "Remember me?"

"Mr Eigerman, you took me to your family. Your Mama, I like. And your sister. Your father, wanted me to go somewhere else."

"He changed his mind."

"Because of your Mama."

"Where did you learn English?"

"I learn in school of my Dobri Bošnjani who die."

"Ifeta, I would like to ask you questions about Adenir Ademović, the man who brought you here."

"He was bad man. He come to our house and shoot Grandpa, Pappa, Mama, Besim and Elvedin, my brothers. Then he take me."

"What made him take you?"

"He say I look like his daughter, Adelais."

"Did Adenir tell you why he came to Belfast?"

"He not tell."

"What happened to Adenir's daughter?"

"I not know. He protect me from other men."

"There was some good in him."

"Like Paul, he come with you to take me away."

"Without Paul, you might not be here."

"Paul, he talk to me, was kind, then they would not let him see me."

"What did they do to you in that house?"

"I am kept by myself. They bring men to see me. I have no clothes when they look at me. They go away, other times they bring more men to look."

"You must have been very frightened."

"Yes, frightened, On the night we have to leave the house because of bomb, they hold a…what you call it when men bid money?"

"An auction."

"Yes, sell me."

I'm concerned about the way she is anwering, and talking about her experiences. Her tone is flat, without inflection, without emotion. I glance at Joshua and I can tell we both know that Ifeta has yet to grieve over her lost family and to weep through the terrifying and terrible things that happened to her.

"Ifeta, would you mind staying with doctor Horowitz a while longer?"

"I am safe here. I stay."

"Good. I won't ask you any more questions."

"Will you come back and see me?"

"Yes, Ifeta, I will."

"Will you bring Paul?"

"If it is possible."

Joshua sees me to the portico. I say, "What's my future mother-in-law like?"

"Your future mother-in-law?"

"When you marry Joanna, she and I will have a mother-in-law. Be *Mishpoche*—family, So, what's our *shviger* like?"

"She prays."

"For you, she has to. For you, we all do."

"*Keyner tsu hern.* (No one to hear) *Shalom.*"

"*Shalom,* Joshua, *Es iz* (There is)."

I drive, wondering if Adenir's body is still in cold storage. I'd like to see what the man looked like. He's in the forensic mortuary.

"Where was he found?" I ask the pathologist.

"In an alleyway between the Falls and the Shankhill. He was shot in the head with .22. The bullet was still in his brain. No other DNA anywhere."

He has no objection of my taking a photograph of his face.

"We've finished with him," the pathologist says, "If nobody claims him in the next month, he'll be cremated."

"I'll see if I can find someone to bury him."

I thank the pathologist. When I leave, I examine my car. I pray: *Adonai, conceal me in your shelter in these days of trouble.* I drive home, lock my car in my garage, make myself a meal, after which I phone Ollie.

I tell him about Ifeta, and about how Adenir Ademović brought her to Belfast and what happened when they arrived.

"You've got a bullet from a .22 from his brain. Find any guns when you arrested those men at the brothel?"

"We found guns."

"See if there's a match. By the way, Adenir came here expecting to get in touch with someone. I'm going to try to find that someone, who might give him a burial. If not, I'll bury him."

"No need to ask why."

"Let's just say I don't like cremations."

31

"Yeshua, I know that fear is a prison, and its bars are thick and wide. Escape is difficult unless I increase my faith in You. My faith is the key that will let me out of this prison growing inside me. Let my faith increase the borders of my abilities and establish my nearness to You. Open my eyes to see your power working, for You shall not leave me in want."

I fire up my computer. Its brain's a bit slow in responding to my fingers dancing on the keyboard, but eventually it tells me I am on the internet.

I ask it a question: How many Eastern Orthodox churches are there in Belfast? It tells me four, and shows me their names, and where they are on a map. I start with the assumption that Adenir was Eastern Orthodox as he took Ifeta to one. Contacting each, I talk with their Bishops and make appointments.

I get to my garage. I find Tony Esposito there with another man.

Tony says, "Open it up."

"What sort of a greeting is that, Tony?"

"Just open the garage door."

"Tony, be a good boy."

"Shut up, open up."

"There must have been a time in your life Tony, when you did the right thing. Remember when that was?"

"Jamesie, get his keys."

"Jamesie, that would be wrong of you."

"Only my friends call me Jamesie."

"I am your friend, Jamesie. I'm trying to save you from doing wrong."

"Get his keys!"

"Tony, when was the last time your mother was proud of you? Jamesie, don't come any nearer."

Jamesie makes a lunge at me. I neatly side-step. He goes past, turns, and makes another lunge. This time as he passes I hit him forceably on back of his neck which throws his medulla into confusion, and puts him down. Tony comes at me. I slice his Adam's apple, and he's on his knees, gasping.

I throw up the garage door, go in and come out with cable ties. Jamesie's vital centres still haven't recovered. I pull his arms behind his back and tie his wrists and ankles. I do the same with Tony. I pull them into the garage, and sit them against the wall.

When I think they can understand, I say, "Well, boys, I'll leave you here because, I have appointments to keep, miles to go, so have a sleep."

I tape their mouths so they can breathe through their noses.

***

The first bishop's name is Nikitas Kavadas. When I explain the situation to him, he is only too willing to help. I show him Adenir's photograph and ask if any of his flock has the name Ademović or had that name before marriage.

He shows me his congregational list, but I draw a blank on that. Bishop Nikitas, says he will check if any of his female flock had the name Ademović before they were married. He doubts it, for he is sure that none of his congregation are from Bosnia. I give him my card and he says he'll get in touch if anyone turns up.

The second bishop, Gregorios Strenopoulos is bean-pole thin, but accomodating, and with him I draw another blank and he too says he'll get in touch if anyone turns up.

Bishop number three is Athenagoras Theocharous and he has the build of an athelete. As before. Also with the fourth bishop, Germanos Kokkinakis. Germanos is the only one who tells me that he will claim Adenir's body himself if no one else does, and lay him to rest according to the rites of the Orthodox Church. I ask him to let me know if that happens.

To the phones of all four bishops, I send a copy of Adenir's photograph.

***

It's near evening. I enter my street and recognise Tony's car. I park. It's locked. I look in, on the back seat there is a coil of rubbber tubing.

Tony and Jamesie are still there when I get my car back in my garage. Their eyes are closed. I kick the soles of their shoes. Jamesie's eyes are bleary. Tony's glare.

I tear the tape from each mouth.

"Glad you stayed boys. I've some questions."

Tony's language is choice.

"Don't be like that, Tony. Who gave the order to kill me?" More choice language.

"Whose idea was it to make my death look like suicide?"

Tony tells me where I can go.

I have the rubber tubing and adhesive tape from Tony's car. I tape the tubing onto the exhaust of my car.

"This is what's called role reversal," I say. "You were supposed to do this to me."

I open the back door of the car, take Jamesie by the feet and drag him to where I put his legs on the back seat, go round and open the other door and pull him in. I don't heed his protests. I do the same with Tony who slips off Jamesie onto the floor.

I close both doors, and put the end of the hose through the window closing it so that it holds the hose in place.

I get in front and lean over to where they're wriggling. I show them my keys.

"These are what you wanted. Now, unless you answer my questions I'll start the engine."

"No! That would be murder," says Jamesie.

"What would it be if you were doing it to me?"

"That's different."

"How is it different, Jamesie?"

"We do it for a living, you're supposed to be some kind of four by two Christian. You're supposed to turn the other cheek."

"That's only when I'm insulted. You two have put my life in danger so I'm allowed to fight back."

"Ah please, mister, don't do this."

"Tell me what I want to know and I won't have to."

"Shut up, Jamesie, he's bluffin'. He ain't gonna gas us."

"Want to take that chance, Tony?"

"Yeah, I reckon you're bluffin'."

"Right," I say. "Who's the mastermind who told you how to kill me?"

"We're sayin' nothin'."

"Do you know, Jamesie?"

"Jamesie's sayin' nothin' too."

I start the engine, then get out and close the door after me.

"Hey, you, mister, come back here!" Jamesie.

"I'll come back in three minutes, if you're still around maybe you'll tell me what I want to know."

"We'll tell you! We'll tell you!"

"I want to hear that from Tony."

Who tells me again where to go.

"I'm leaving," I say.

I hear them start to cough. I turn out the light.

"When you're dead," I say. "You're going to have one hell of an afterlife."

I'm not sure just how long it takes carbon monoxide to cause unconsciousness or death. I think I've really got myself into a worrying situation, when Tony coughs out: "I'll talk! I'll talk." I breath a sigh of relief, turn on the light, turn off the engine, and drag them out of the car. I partly open the garage door to let the air dissipate the fumes from the exhaust.

32

"All right Tony, whose idea was it to arrange my death as a suicide?"

"I got a headache," Tony says.

"It can be made worse."

"It was Sammy's. Sammy Payne."

"Let's get you both back in the car."

"It wasn't Sammy, mister. Tony and me ain't with Sammy no more."

"Why not, Jamesie?"

"He took a dislike to Tony, didn't trust him no more."

"That was your fault," Tony says.

"So who are you working for now?"

"Tell him, Tony."

"Shut up, Jamesie. I'll tell him without you tellin' me to tell him."

"Tell me the truth, Tony."

"Dennie Armstrong."

Dennis Victor Armstrong, brought in and questioned about a number of murders, never charged.

"Why woud he want me dead?"

"He never said."

"Who gives him orders?"

"No, idea. My head's hurtin'."

"So's mine," says Jamesie.

"Know what I think? I think Sammy's dead."

"What makes you think he's dead?"

"I think Dennie Armstrong's taken over. Where do you bury your dead and the missing?"

"You'll find out someday."

"Know where Steven Ford is buried?"

"I'm no undertaker."

"Do you know, Jamesie?"

"I don't know nothin'."

"Time for the car again."

"No mister, I can't tell you nothin'."

"What about you Tony, you want to tell me anything more, like who's really behind all of your criminal activities?"

"Ask Dennie."

"Which pocket are your car keys in?"

"What you want to know for?"

"You look like death warmed up, you need oxygen. I'm taking you both to hospital."

"Let us go, and we'll come after you."

I free their ankles. "Stand up. Let's see if you can walk."

They got to their feet rather shakily.

"Let's walk to your car. I'm going to drive, so where are your keys?"

He told me, and I got them.

"What about these ties?"

"Later," I say.

When I get them to Tony's car, I put them in the back seat. As I drive I say,

"You've been gassed with carbon monoxide. Now I've heard that even after you've survived, there's still danger of you stopping breathing and dying. It's rare but it sometimes happens, so when I take you to hospital tell the doctor about the carbon monoxide."

"What if he wants to know how we got gassed?"

"You'll think of something. Just remember I've got everything you've told me recorded on my phone."

"I didn't see you doin' that."

"You weren't meant to."

I get to the hospital, and use the drop-off bay. There's not too many people around and when I get Tony and Jamesie to the door of A&E, I cut the wrist ties.

"In you go." I prod them through the door.

"What about my car keys?"

"Call a taxi."

I drive back to my garage, open the door, and the doors of my car to allow any carbon monoxide to dissipate. I take the tubing from the exhaust.

I leave Tony's car in a car park about a mile away, on my walk back home I buy a take-away.

33

Next day, when I get to my office, Elsie, at ground floor reception tells me a woman came earlier and left a package for me and and said to tell me it was a present for loving her. I'm pretty sure it's not a bomb, and it's from Julie Maynes.

I take it and now I'm absorbed in reading the life and times of Jimmie Maynes.

Julie's note tells me she's talked with Adam and they're reconciled. She hopes things go well with me, and that her father's journals help.

They do, indeed.

Jimmy Maynes ordered the killing of Patrick Ford, the order coming down to Maynes from Robert Seymore, and executed by John Blair.

Robert Seymore, father of Laurence Seymore, leader of the Progressive Socialist Party, member of the Assembly, owner of numerous *Rest Easy* hotels.

Maynes was also ordered to arrange the killing of Steven Ford. The two men Maynes chose were Dennie Armstrong and Laurence Seymore.

34

For nothing is hidden that will not be disclosed, nothing is covered up that will not be known and come out into the open.

I scan Jimmy Mayne's journal on my printer and save it on my computer. I send copies to Ollie's and Jo-Jo's computers. and I put a copy on each of two memory sticks and put them in addressed envelopes.

Mayne's journal names a number of corrupt police officers, some dead, some living, some still in PSNI service.

Maynes found out more than he was supposed to about the men grazing the top meadow of East Side organised crime.

Robert Seymore died last year, but his syndicate lives on in all its corruption.

Jo-Jo arrives. She looks determined.

"I've a bone to pick with you, Stan."

"Must be a lot of meat on it, Jo-Jo."

"What have you been saying to Joshua?"

"I'm sure he told you."

"He did."

"Then, why ask?"

"I want to hear it from you."

"I'm not going to hinder you marrying Joshua. I'm not going to hinder the two of you adopting Ifeta, if you think that's the best thing for her. The choices and the responsibilities are yours."

"Joshua is having second thoughts about us adopting Ifeta. Because of what you said to him."

"Quite possibly. I said what I had to say. I don't take back a word of it."

"Well, good for you! Who are you to say what we should or shouldn't do!"

"Joshua and you are the ones to talk this through and decide what is best for Ifeta. Ifeta comes from believers who call themselves Krstjani—Christians. They are neither Roman Catholic nor Eastern Orthodox. Just believers in Jesus as their Messiah, same as myself."

"You and Joshua will have to deal with that belief, and decide whether or not you have enough love to do so. I only point out the possibility of problems that might arise."

"It's interference."

"Call it what you like. Talk it over with Joshua in a way that both of you can consider the consequences for the three of you if you adopt Ifeta."

"What consequences?"

"You'll figure it out, Jo-Jo. Shalom?"

After a silence: "Shalom, Stan."

I tell Joanna about Mayne's journal and how I scanned it to my comupter.

"I sent you and Ollie a copy if anything happens to me and Ollie."

"You mean if you're killed?"

"I mean anything."

"Go to the police with that journal."

"When the time is ripe."

"What are you going to do?"

"See a murderer in high places."

35

Even if I pass through death-dark ravines, I will fear no disaster; for you are with me; your rod and staff reassure me.

In the centre of Belfast, there's a late Victorian building, now transformed into a multi-partitioned rabbit hutch for tourists; a *'Rest Easy'* hotel; the heart of Laurence Seymore's empire where as an elected member of our assembly he holds his political surgery. I telephone to say I'm coming.

I'm patted down by a hefty minder. Another openes a door for me and I pass into the presence of the honourable member.

"I've been expecting you," he says.

"You thought I'd never get here."

"I truly didn't think you'd make it."

"You just can't rely on the help nowadays."

"That's true."

"You know why I'm here."

"I do."

"So, tell me the whereabouts of Steven Ford's remains."

"What makes you think I would know that?"

"Steven is where you and Dennie Armstrong put him."

"You're talking through your hat."

"I'm not wearing a hat. Mary Ford wants you to know she forgives you and Dennie, for murdering her son. Do the right thing and let Mary know where Stevens remains are."

"Don't know what you're talking about."

"You've come up in the world since Jimmy Maynes sent you and Dennie to protect your father's interests."

"If you want to go out the way you came in, you should leave."

"Beautiful accent you have Laurence, Cambridge? Lovely. All bought and paid for by the immorality of your father. He was a sinful man, Laurence, just as you are a sinful man, laundering illegal monies through your hotels."

"This is your last chance to leave."

"I know you don't want to kill me here, so I'll stay. Where did you put Steven's body."

"You've just dug yourself a grave."

"Tell me, it'll be good for your soul."

"You're a dead man walking."

"So tell me. Where did you and Dennie hide Steven's body?"

"How'd you find out?"

"Same way an archaeologist discovers the past. Just gently scrape away the corruption, layer by layer, and we come to Dennie, Jimmy, Sammy, your father and yourself."

"But how'd you know I was with Dennie that night?"

"Doesn't matter, you were. So tell me, where did you take Steven?"

"We took him to an undertakers."

"Which one."

"A friendly one."

"Come on, give me a name. What harm can it do if I'm a dead man walking?"

"It's good you realise it. Salem Jones."

"Go on."

"He had a body to bury. We put your man in along with it."

"What was the name of the corpse?"

"Don't remember."

"Remember what day it was?"

"Thursday, 24th of August."

"What cemetry?"

"Haven't a clue. And you won't be around to ask the undertaker."

"Was it you or Dennie killed Steven?"

"I killed him."

"You say that with such pride."

"He told us all he knew. Which wasn't much."

"Laurence, my heart goes out to you. I'm going to give you a chance. Have a change of heart. Stop working for evil and start working for good. You're going to meet your maker and have to answer for all the harm you've done in this world."

"Both my makers are dead and buried. You can believe there's a big maker up there in the sky, but there ain't, so nothin's goin' to judge me."

"Well, Laurence, I commit you into the hands of the God you don't believe in. I advise you to repent before you see Him."

He presses a buzzer on his desk, says, "Send in Willy and Tom." The door opens and two rather large men come in.

"See if he's wearing a wire, or if his phone has been on record."

Their search is rough and thorough. At the end of it I say, "See, no wire. No phone. No wallet. No recorder."

"Take this man a long distance, and make sure he doesn't come back."

"I'm sorry for you, " I say. "You can still reconsider and change your life."

"Get him out of here."

36

Thomas and William take me out a back way, and put me in a car. Thomas drives, William sits with me in the back.

"William, no need to be anxious, I'm not armed."

"Shut up, you."

"My name's Stanley by the way. Thomas, where are you taking me?"

"He told you to shut up."

"He did, but why should I? If you're going to kill me, I'd like to know where you're going to do it."

"We don't want to hear you," says William.

"I wish you no harm but, after all, you're about to kill yourselves."

"You got it wrong, it's you we're goin' to kill."

"But if you kill me, it is you who will die."

"You're nuts," says Thomas. "You're the one who'll die."

"No, Thomas, kill me and I will live, it is you and William who will die."

"That's all backside foremost, now shut your gub."

"Thomas and William, do you think Laurance Seymore loves you?"

"Come off it, don't be soft. He's not like that."

"What I mean is, does he have any great regard for your well being? Does he hold you in such regard that he would risk dying to save you, if you were wounded in a battle with the police?"

"He'd do what we'd do, get off side, and save our skins."

"So, he has no love for you, and you have no love for him."

"You can say that again."

"Then why are you ready to die for him by committing murder on his say so?"

"He pays well," says William.

"So, you're dying for him, for money, and not for love?"

"Listen mister, it's you who's goin' to die, not us."

"Where were you born and bred, Thomas?"

"The Hammer."

"What about you, William?"

"I'm from the 'Nick', just across the road."

"So, from the Shankill. You've both been to Sunday School."

"Yeah, I've been."

"Me too."

"Good to know," I say.

"What's good to know?"

"It's good to know that my two murderers, Thomas and William, have been to Sunday School, and know that God says they shouldn't kill anyone, and they know that God sent His Son to die on a cross, not for money but for love, to save their two souls, and, if they stopped murdering people and believed in Him they could leave Lawrence Seymore's organisation and join His for ever; now and after they die."

"Shut your face," says Thomas. "Here we are."

"Yes," says William, "We're here."

"Well," I say. "If this is where you're going to kill me, I want you to know that I forgive you this terrible sin."

37

We've crossed the border and are in the Republic of Ireland. I'm wondering whether I'll see snow again, all over Ireland, falling on every part of the dark central plain, on treeless hills, falling softly upon the Bog of Allen and on Shannon waves. Would I ever again read Joyce.

"Sit there," Thomas says. He looks over his shoulder at William, and says, "Come on," with a directive nod of his head and gets out of the car. William gets out and the two stand at the front of the car where I can see them talking.

Their talk becomes animated with much hand gestures, and head noddings, and jerkings.

They come back to the car, but instead of taking me out, get in.

"Stanley," says Thomas.

I think if they're going to kill me they wouldn't be calling me Stanley, but all sorts of bad names, in foul language, to make me less than human.

"Any money on you? Any credit cards?"

"Not a bean, you know I got empty pockets," I say.

Thomas looks at William as if wondering what to do. William nods to Thomas and Thomas says, "We're taking you to Dublin Airport."

"Not a quiet spot," I say.

"We don't want you walkin' home."

"You don't?"

"You'll be flyin'."

"How?"

"We'll oil your armpits."

"Shut up, Willy. We'll loan you money for a ticket."

"That's very good of you, but I'm concerned about you. What are you going to tell your Seymore?"

"Nothin'. We're goin' to disappear, and when he sees you back there, it'll look like you knocked us off."

"I'll pay you back. Let me know where to send the money."

"No," says William. "We're not goin' to let anybody know where we are."

"Consider it a gift," says Thomas.

"All I can say is 'thank you'. You're on your way to God's Kingdom, but be sure to enter it without your guns."

We turn off at Junction Two, and when we reach the airport Thomas uses his credit card and buys me a flight to Belfast. We sit down at a coffee bar next to a Catholic priest.

"Boys," I say. "I owe you my life, but would you do one more thing for me?"

"What's that?"

"Write a declaration that Laurance Seymore ordered you to kill me, but instead of that, you let me go. And sign it."

"We don't want to be brought back to court."

"You won't be."

"You sure?"

"I'm sure."

William buys paper and pens and they write. I've talked loud enough for the Catholic priest to hear, and when they've finished I ask him to witness their signatures.

"He won't tell," I say. "Do you swear that what you have written is the truth, the whole truth and nothing but the truth?"

Each said it was. I ask the Catholic priest if he would read their statements and witness their signatures.

"You heard them swear to the truth?" I say.

"I heard."

"Thomas and William are afraid that you'll tell the police on them."

"These are confessions, I can't say about anything given me as a confession. Do you want absolution?"

"We're Prods, and we're goin'."

I shake their hands, and when they've gone I thank the Priest.

"Most unusual," he says.

"You don't know the half of it," I say.

I have a two hour wait.

"May I borrow your phone?" I ask the priest.

"Why not?" I take it and phone Ollie.

"Where are you?" he wants to know. "Joanna's worried about you."

"Dublin Airport, safe and sound. Explain later. Ollie," I tell him where my car is parked, "take the two envelopes addressed to the television stations and if you would, hand them in personally."

"Copies of the one you sent me?"

"Just so."

"Yeah, its time to do that?"

"Keys are taped under rear mudguard."

"Speak with Joanna."

"I will."

"May I make another call? Thank you." I get Jo-Jo.

"Are you all right? Ima's worried, she's been phoning you and getting no answer."

"Tell Ima I'm fine, and on my way home from Dublin Airport."

"Are you hurt?"

"No."

"When I gave Oliver that stick, he said you were a fool to go without back-up."

"That's Ollie. All things worked together for good."

"It's not turning out so good for Joshua and me."

"Oh?"

"You might well say, 'Oh', as if you're surprised. He said that it might not be such a good idea for us to adopt Ifeta."

"What did you say to that?"

"That it might not be such a good idea for us to be married."

"To which he replied?"

"He was thinking that as well."

"Cooled down?"

"Yes."

"Has he?"

"I hope so."

"So you can discuss?"

"Like adults."

"See you all later, Jo-Jo."

I thank the priest.

"You seem to lead an interesting life."

"All in the name of Adonai, Yeshua, and *rauch Hakodesh.*"

"Ha! Or as I would say: *In nomine Patris et Filii, et Spiritus Sancti.*"

"Amen to that."

It's evening when I arrive in Belfast. I take the bus into the centre and collect my car. The two letters are no longer there. I drive home.

First thing I do is to go to my room, fall on my knees.

Adonai, Yeshua, and ruach Hakodesh thank you for my deliverance this day. Yeshua, you said that without Adonai, you could do nothing in your own will while you dwelt among us, and I can do nothing in my own will without you while I dwell here.

Thank you for the words you gave me this day, and for Thomas and William, Yeshua, Lord, let Your Spirit lead them into your Kingdom so that they may dwell among us. I pray also for Laurence Seymore, and Dennie Armstrong. Let them be aware of, and in dire need of, your saving grace. Pray to your father Lord Yeshua, for all concerned, for Adonai is the One who saves those whom He saves and rejects those whom He rejects. Let your Spirit hover over Jo-Jo, Joshua and Ifeta. In your name, I ask these things of Adonai.

38

Keep asking, and it will be given to you; keep seeking, and you will find; keep knocking, and the door will be opened to you. For everyone who keeps asking receives; he who keeps seeking finds; and to him who keeps knocking, the door will be opened.

It's nearly 10am when I wake. After breakfast, I phone Ollie who says,
"Let us meet."
"My office, Ollie."
On my way, I buy a bunch of flowers which I give to Elsie.
"They're lovely. What are they for?"
"For the times you become my unofficial secretary."
"Inspector Black's waiting for you."
With jam doughnuts.
"Knew you'd have the coffee and nothing else."
"That's what being a policeman does for you."
"So, tell the tale."
I give Ollie a recital from the time I went to see Laurence Semour to the time I phoned him from Dublin airport. He didn't speak until I'd finished.
"The officers mentioned are now subject to internal affairs. Seymore and Armstrong have been arrested along with a number of NIFF members mentioned by Maynes."
"All to the good."
"I'll deal with the undertaker because, if what Seymore said is true, we need lawful permission to exhume the body. A licence from the Ministry of Justice. I'll see to all that. You'll be a witness against Seymore."
"He thinks I'm dead."
"All the better."
"Thomas and William will be long gone."
"Their affidavits will do. I'll go see the undertaker."

39

I'm still in my office when Ima arrives. She sees what's left of the doughnuts and coffee.

"Oiii! With junk food my son ruins his figure."

"A doughnut now and then, Ima."

"That box holds six."

"Ollie was here."

"Oi vey! Three each they have."

"Ima, why are you here?"

"Here I am to see if my son the detective lives. Yesterday, all day, I phone. No answer I get. Your sister, my daughter, tells me nothing, except not to worry. To tell me not to worry means I worry. I go out with that nice lady, Mary, and she has not heard from you either. This you give us both to worry about."

"I am alive and well, Ima."

"And eating doughnuts, yet. Round the corner is diabetes."

"You eat sugars too, Ima. I should worry about you."

"For me to eat sugars is different."

"I should have such an Ima."

"And such an Ima you should worry about. A son who gives me to read the *B'rit Hadashah*."

"Ha! Yeshua gives you food for thought."

"And not sugary it is. Your poor father, what will he do?"

"What's happening?"

"To me he is the best of husbands, but…"

"But?"

"I, your mother ask, can I come and live with you?"

"Why? What has Abba done?"

"Nothing. Can you put me up?"

"My appartment is small."

"I have money. A house for you I buy, we will live together."

"Why? Has Abba shown you the door?"

"No, but in the *B'rit Hadashah,* Adonai says I must listen to His Son."

"Where in the *B'rit Hadashah* does it say that?"

"I show you." Ima takes her phone with the *B'rit Hadashah* on it. Shows me. "There, Yeshua's on the mountain with Kefa, Ya'akov and Yochanan and they see Moshe and Eliyahue, then they see them no more only Yeshua. Adonai tells them that Yeshua is His Son and that they are to listen to what he says."

"How does that tell you that you must leave Abba?"

"My eyes are opened to a wonderful thing. Look! Look what it says here:

'This is why the Father loves me: because I lay down my life in order to take it up again! No one takes it away from me; on the contrary, I lay it down of my own free will. I have the power to lay it down, and I have the power to take it up again. This is what my Father commanded me to do.'

Do you see what this means?"

"Tell me."

"Yeshua is in that garden, full of fear. His Abba has told Him what to do. When Adam was in the garden, Adonai told him what to do, but do it, he did not, and a mess is the world.

To clean up the mess Adonai sends Yeshua. Yeshua. doesn't want to do what His Abba wants. But if He is disobedient like Adam, a worse mess is the world. The damage Adam has done, Yeshua repairs, and His Abba loves him for it."

"Know why I love you, Ima?"

"My son will tell me."

"Because you first loved me. Without your love and Abba's I would not know how to love. The same is true of Adonai, Yeshua and His Holy Spirit because of their love for each other and for us, we would not know how to love them."

"Oy! I am to love Yeshua, but what about Abba? Adonai, tells me I must listen to his Son, Yeshua. Abba, I have not yet told that I know Messiah is Yeshua. What will happen when I do? I, your Abba, will have to leave."

"Let me read you what Yeshua says:

'To those who are married I have a command, and it is not from me but from the Lord: a woman is not to separate herself from her husband. But if she does

separate herself, she is to remain single or be reconciled with her husband. Also, a husband is not to leave his wife. To the rest I say—I, not the Lord: if any brother has a wife who is not a believer, and she is satisfied to go on living with him, he should not leave her. Also, if any woman has an unbelieving husband who is satisfied to go on living with her, she is not to leave him. For the unbelieving husband has been set aside for God by the wife, and the unbelieving wife has been set aside for God by the husband but as it is, they are set aside for God. But if the unbelieving spouse separates himself, let him be separated. In circumstances like these, the brother or sister is not enslaved—God has called you to a life of peace. For how do you know, wife, whether you will save your husband? Or how do you know, husband, whether you will save your wife?'"

Ima gets up, walks around my office, takes her time.

"I tell Abba, and we see."

40

Ima and I pray together, then she leaves. I get a text from Ollie, saying I can see Laurence Seymore any time I'm ready.

I phone Mary.

"Mary, progress report. How about I pick you up for lunch?"

This time we go to a restaurant along the Lagan near one of the locks. It's peaceful and conversations are muted. When we finish our main, and order our desert, I say, "Mary, we know who the two were who abducted Steven. They're in custody. You still want to talk to them?"

"Who are they?"

"Laurence Seymore and Dennis Armstrong."

"The politician?"

"The same, and the leader of NIFF."

"You're sure it's them?"

"Certain."

"You've spoken to them?"

"Only to Seymore. He told me."

"Seemed a stupid thing for him to do."

"He thought I wouldn't live to tell the tale."

Mary said nothing until, "Did he tell you where Steven is?"

"More or less. He told me what he did, and from that information we can find Steven."

"Are you sure he told you the truth?"

"He thinks I'm dead. Yes, I think he told me the truth."

"Then I want to see both of them. Together if possible?"

"We have permission to visit Seymore. I'll just check with Ollie about Armstrong."

I text Ollie, our desert comes. I get a reply during coffee.

"It's fine, Mary, tomorrow afternoon."

***

At the holding station where Seymore and Armstrong are, I tell Mary that Ollie will be with her, but I'll wait until I've heard what they say.

We are met by Ollie. He tells us that Salem Jones, the retired undertaker, has an alert mind, and a good memory for what happened to Steven when he was forced him to bury him in the same coffin as the remains of Mr Henry Woodburn. A couple more signatures then we can exhume, and open the coffin.

"Why didn't he go to the police?" Mary asks.

"They threatened to torch his business and harm his family."

"What will happen to him?"

"At his age, nothing."

They go to the interview room and sit, I stay where I can see and hear from behind one-way glass. Seymore and Armstrong are brought in handcuffed. Their legal representative comes in.

Seymore looks at Mary. "Who is she, and why's she here?"

Ollie says, "This meeting is off the record, and the lady is Mrs Ford. Mrs Ford, this is Mr Adams representing both Mr Seymore and Mr Armstrong."

"Mr Seymore," Mary says, "And Mr Armstrong. You two boys murdered my son, Steven."

"How can you say that Mrs Ford?"Adams asks. "My clients deny such an allegation."

"Mr Seymore told Stanley Eigerman they did."

"It's a lie, I've never met Eigerman."

"Please do not tell any more lies," Mary says, "I want you both to know, that I forgive you for taking the life of my son. Especially you Mr Seymore who pulled the trigger. I hope you ask God to forgive you for that sin, and for the hurt and anguish you caused me."

Seymore: "It's really terrible what happened to your son, Mrs Ford. I know how you must feel, but it wasn't us."

"After you killed Steven, you took him to Mr Jones the undertaker, and forced him bury Steven along with the body of Mr Henry Woodburn."

"Mrs Ford is there any proof of what you are saying."

"The fact is, Mr Adams, Mr Seymore told Mr Eigerman before he sent him out with two men, Thomas and William, to be killed."

"I don't know what she's talking about."

"Oh yes you do, Laurence," I say coming into the room. "Why don't we just say that I am living proof."

"Why Mr Eigerman, it's good to see you. Now that you're here why don't you tell this poor lady who has all this time been grieving for her son, that you've be leading her up the garden path with these stories about Mr Armstrong and myself having murdered her son."

"Ah, Laurence," I say, "you have the cheek of the devil, but you haven't a leg to stand on."

"Mrs Ford, he came to see me with the purpose of blackmailing myself, and Mr Armstrong. I had two of my men show him out."

"A man you say you've never met, Mr Seymore?" Mary says.

I continue, "Thomas and William. They drove me over the border. You won't be seeing them again, Laurence. They drove me over the border to dispose of my body in some bog. Instead we all had something to eat with a Catholic priest. They gave me affidavits written and sworn in the presence of Father O'Rourke, who witnessed their signatures, and then they went off to a new life elsewhere."

Ollie produced the affidavits, read them aloud. "These will stand up in a court of law." He handed them to Mr Adams. "Wouldn't you say so?"

"It certainly corroborates Mr Eigerman's testimony."

"Mrs Ford," Ollie says. "Have you anthing further to say to these men?"

"Only this," Mary says. "Both of you at the moment are full of sin. You need to do something about that. I hope you do."

"Eigerman, one way or another, your days are numbered," Laurence says.

"I'm sorry you feel that way. It's not a good way to feel. It's self-destructive."

We leave. Adams stays behind with his clients.

41

Ollie says, "Take his threat seriously, Stanley."

"Yes, Ollie."

"He won't want us, including you Mary, testifying against him."

"I know."

"I'll let you know when the exhumation is to take place."

"Good."

"Mary, here's my card. You need me, call me. I don't think those men will be asking God to forgive them."

"I hope you're wrong Ollie."

"Stanley will see you home. Take care."

"You too, Ollie."

I drive Mary home.

"Come in," she says, "I'll make us something."

This I help her to do.

"How will they know it's Steven?"

"You'll give a DNA sample."

"Will they be able to tell after all this time?"

"They'll be able to tell. We need to talk about your safety."

"Am I in that much danger?"

"We are. You, Ollie, myself. I've thought of a way to keep you safe."

"What about you and Ollie? I hope he doesn't mind me calling him Ollie."

"He loves it. We'll find a way to do good to those who would do us evil."

"What's this way you've thought of protecting me?"

"I'll tell you tomorrow. Stay in until I come, and don't open the door to anyone but me."

***

"And you're quite certain the remains will be those of Steven?" Jean says.

"I'm sure."

"What do you say, Steven?"

"If Stan says Grandma's in danger, then we must help."

"Stan, you'll have to tell her about us," Jean says.

"I'll let her know."

"What will she think of me, denying her a grandson all these years."

"Be surprised if she didn't thank you for looking after him so well."

"When you tell her, Stan…"

"I'll say words Yeshua will give me, to ears that Yeshua will bless. Can you give me a recent photograph of Steven?"

"Of course."

"I don't think they'll find Mary here, but if they do you and Steven will be in danger."

"It's a bridge to cross if we come to it."

"Jean," I say, "you're a woman after my own heart."

"What makes you think I'm after your heart?"

"I hoped."

When I get back from Jean's. I phone Mary and tell her I'll see her first thing in the morning to tell her about the arrangements I've made. I phone Ollie. He tells me the exhumation will take place tomorrow night.

I go to bed, but cannot sleep because I'm excited, not in expectation of danger, but because of emotions, I have not felt, since I first saw my departed Ruth; a feeling of loving excitement, with tremulous feelings of desire.

Steven had said,

"Keep hoping, Stan, I know she likes you."

Jean said, "Steven! How you make your mother blush."

I said, "And how you make me blush."

Jean and I stood looking at each other with a certain amount of confusion.

"Ha!" said Steven, "I'll leave." Steven departed, smiling.

"Is it true, Jean?"

"What?"

"That you like me?"

"Of course I like you."

"If, when all this is over, and all is well, would…ah…?"

"…I like you more than I do?"

"Yes."

"Aren't we a little too old for this?"

"If you feel the way I feel right now, we're not too old."

"Then I'll walk out with you, as we say in the country." She extended her hands towards me and I took them in mine. We stood there for I don't know how long, holding hands, until Jean said, "You must go."

And I said, "Yes, I must."

I'm in a quandry Lord Yeshua. We seem such an unlikely couple; a farmer and a private detective. How will it possibly work? Without you it won't work.

I spend an hour sighing, before I fall asleep.

42

I wake up in the morning with these words ringing in my ears:

For now we see obscurely in a mirror, but then it will be face to face. Now I know partly; then I will know fully, just as God has fully known me. But for now, three things last—trust, hope, love; and the greatest of these is love. Pursue love!

I ask Adonai, Yeshua, and the Holy Spirit to give me loving words to speak to Mary.

I arrive with a technician who departs, taking with him a DNA sample from Mary, I say,

"I've arranged a place of safety for you Mary, but first I have something to tell you that may come as a surprise, and at the same time, be something of a shock."

We sit down and I tell her how I found Jean McBride, the girl Steven took to the pictures, and how, when I went to see her I got the surprise of my life. I give her the photograph of her grandson.

"She kept this photograph of Steven?"

"The young man in the photo is called Steven, but he is not Steven, your son, he is your grandson, Steven."

Mary sits holding the photograph.

"He looks so much like Steven."

"He does, Mary. He wants to see you, and so does, Jean."

"Why didn't she let me know before this?"

"You can ask her that. You'll be staying with them at their farm."

"She never married?"

"No. It was their intention to marry. Jean brought Steven up within her own family."

"Oh, why didn't she come and tell me when she was pregnant?"

"Maybe it was best Steven was brought up on a farm, than in this troubled city."

"You see God's hand in this?"

"I see the hand of Adonai in everything."

"Are they willing to have me?"

"Only too willing. Especially Steven, he's looking forward to meeting his grandmother."

"When do you want me to go?"

"Just as soon as you gather up the things you'll need for an enjoyable stay in the country."

"Enjoyable?"

"What else should it be?"

On the way Mary says, "I think you're fond of Jean."

"I won't deny it."

"I can tell from the tender way you say her name."

"Tender is right."

"And how does Jean say your name?"

"Warmly."

"Warmly is right, too."

"When all this is over…"

"You don't have to tell me."

Jean and Steven are there to meet us.

I help Mary from the car and we all come together.

"Mary, this is Jean and Steven." The words are hardly out of my mouth when Mary and Jean are in each other's arms weeping, murmuring, patting.

Adonai only knows what thoughts, images and emotions are involved in this embracing of these two women. I just thank Yeshua, and *ruach Hakodesh* for the grace with which Jean, takes Steven's hand and Mary's, and brings them together.

Grandmother and Grandson stand looking at one another then a sudden embrace.

"I'll bring the cases," I say, and when I have them, I bring them into the house.

"I must go," I say.

"Won't you stay a while?" Jean says. "Eat with us."

"I have to get back to Ollie. The exhumation is tonight."

"At least have a cup of tea."

"Well, just a cup of tea."

Steven and his grandmother are in joyful conversation.

"Thank you, Stan, for paving the way."

"For that, thank Adonai."

"I do thank God, but I also thank you."

When I say good-bye to Mary and Steven, Jean sees me to the car.

"Take care, Stan," she says.

"I'll be back tomorrow, Jean. Look after that lady who might have been your mother-in-law."

"I wonder what it would be like having a mother-in-law."

"If you want to find out, I can provide you with a Jewish one?"

"A Jewish one would be nice."

Jean kisses me. I drive away happy.

43

Many of those sleeping in the dust of the earth will awaken, some to everlasting life and some to everlasting shame and abhorrence. But those who can discern will shine like the brightness of heaven's dome, and those who turn many to righteousness like the stars forever and ever.

It's one in the morning and Ollie and I watch the coffin come up from the grave. With due reverence, the lid is taken off and there are two skeletons. The lid is replaced, and the coffin carried to the hearse. We follow as it is driven to the forensic laboratory where the skeletons are removed.

"Well, Stanley, nothing more we can do here."

"Take care, Ollie, I hear you've got a new Chief Constable."

"James Bruce. A Scot, Edinburgh born and bred, speaks purist English."

"But, is he sympathetic to truth?"

"I'd say so. You've spirited Mary away to safety?"

"I'm going back later. I'll stay with her, you can let me know if one of those remains is Steven's."

"Still say you need a gun."

"Still say 'no'."

I drive home, lock up my car, and go to bed. I sleep for three hours, get up, pack a case, and head for the country.

I arrive as they're having breakfast. Mary asks, "Did all go well?"

"It did. There were two in one coffin."

"Were there any clothes?"

"Shrouds."

"What do you think?"

"I think one will be Steven. We'll have to wait and see."

"How long?"

"One, two days."

"It's just…I suppose I can wait that long."

"Jean," I say. "I'd like to stay here until Ollie phones with the result. Can you put up with me, for that length of time?"

"Well, there's room in the hen house. What do you say, Steven?"

"He'd be warmer with the cows."

"True, and I don't think they'd object as much as the hens."

"Cows it is then," I say. "Is there an empty stall?"

"You can have the one next to Steven. I'll have it made up for you."

"Thanks Jean. If there's anything I can do around the farm, just let me know."

"Well," says Steven, "You can give me a hand."

"Not that tree again," says Jean.

"I don't want to plough round it."

"He's taking advantage, Stan."

"I don't mind."

"You will when you see the tree. And you can't go to that field with those town shoes. What size?"

"Eleven."

She leaves the kitchen and comes back with a pair rubber boots.

"Eleven."

"Thank you." I put them on, stamp. "Perfect."

"Right, Stan." Steven is half way through the door. I wave to Jean and Mary as I follow.

We arrive at the field with a tractor driven by Steven and myself in a trailer with tools to take down a tree; chainsaw, handsaw, picks, a long crowbar, a long-tailed shovel, spade, ropes, gloves, and ear muffs.

It's a three acre field clear except for a hawthorn tree standing right in the middle.

Steven stops the tractor. "That's the tree,"

"I got the impression your mother wasn't all that happy about you and this tree."

"It's my neighbour in the next farm, he maintains it's a fairy thorn and should be left to the fairies. In fact, he wanted to buy the field from us so that the fairies would leave us all in peace. Mum doesn't want to make an enemy of Mr Adgee."

"You've decided to take the risk."

"I'm sceptical about what he says."

"So, down it comes."

"Ever use a chain saw?"

"Never."

"Always a first time."

We drive nearer to the tree and unload.

"Plenty of room for it to fall."

I gauge its height. "You'll have to move the tractor."

"No. You'll make it fall the other way."

"Me?"

"You, and the chainsaw."

"I'm to cut down this fairy tree, so the fairies'll get mad at me."

"A precaution."

"What do I do?"

"Take a good wedge-shaped piece from the side away from the tractor, then come round to the tractor side, cut towards it, and the tree will fall away from you."

"Do I shout 'Timber'?"

I leave my coat at the tractor, roll up my sleves, adjust ear muffs and put on gloves as the chainsaw roars into life.

Under Steven's guidance I take out a sizable wedge.

We put the rope around the tree, and Steven reckons the length of the fall, takes the two ends, then tells me to start cutting.

I power the saw again, and cut as he told me, he pulls on the rope until my cutting meets the wedge, and the tree falls, its top about a foot from where he stands.

Steven says, "Your job now is to cut the tree up. Leave the leafy bits for gaps in the hedge."

I begin cutting. Steven digs all around the stump, exposing the roots.

When we stop for lunch, Steven says,

"Stan, I want to talk to you." He's brought shandy in a flask and sandwiches.

"What about?"

"About you and Mum."

44

We sit side by side on the ground, our backs sharing the large tractor wheel.
"Go on, Steven."
"Mum's in love with you."
"And I'm in love with your mother."
"Do you intend to marry her?"
"Yes."
"You don't know each other. Mum's a farmer, and you're a detective."
"We have Yeshua in common, Steven."
"I know, but what good's that if you won't be together."
"Who says we won't be together?"
"You'll be off…detecting."
"That's something your mother and I will work out."
"Think about it." He gets up.
"Let's get back to work. We'll have this stump out before tea time."

Steven cuts roots then tries to move the stump with the crow bar, finds more roots and we dig deeper to get at them. When the stump is free of roots, we pull it out with the tractor.

45

If one of you has a slave tending the sheep or plowing, when he comes back from the field, will you say to him, 'Come along now, sit down and eat'? No, you'll say, 'Get my supper ready, dress for work, and serve me until I have finished eating and drinking; after that, you may eat and drink.' Does he thank the slave because he did what he was told to do? No! It's the same with you—when you have done everything you were told to do, you should be saying, 'We're just ordinary slaves, we have only done our duty.'

In the evening, Jean and I walk along a country lane.

There are things I want to say but don't know how to start.

"Stan…"

"Jean…"

Together.

"You first, Jean."

"How did you like working with Steven?"

"It was good, threw me in at the deep end with that chainsaw, broke the sweat on me."

"He's a hard task master. We have trouble keeping farm labourers."

"He took me to task today over you."

"Me?"

"Protecting his mother."

"What did he say?"

"Said you were in love with me and asked if I was in love with you."

"That was direct, enough. I am. Are you?"

"I am. Asked if I was going to marry you. I said yes."

"When are you going to ask me?"

"Right now, Jean."

"This minute?"

"Will you marry me, Jean."

"This farmer wants a husband. Yes, I'll marry you, Stan."

"How about a kiss in a country lane?"

"I thought you'd never think of it."

"A fine romance."

"With no kisses. Do you dance?"

"Not as good as Fred Astaire."

"But you can Tango?"

"Takes two."

We walk on.

"Steven thinks we're going to have difficulties. You being a farmer, and me being Philip Marlowe."

"Who's Philip Marlowe?"

"A Private Eye with the imagination of Raymond Chandler."

"Like Poirot?"

"Nothing like. His little grey cells belong to Agatha Christie."

"But you're flesh and blood, not just words on paper."

"I am that. We'll get to know each other Jean. I told Steven we had Yeshua in common."

"Jesus is enough provided we're His servants and not volunteers."

"What do you mean?"

"Jesus expects us to be servants, on call to do his will. Volunteers just make Him tea whenever they feel like it, and go according to their own will the rest of the time."

"Half time I don't know if I'm a servant or a volunteer."

"I'm the same."

"How do you understand the *ruach Hakodesh,* Jean*?*"

"The what?"

"God's Holy Spirit."

"It's what leads us."

"You see His Spirit as an 'It'?"

"Don't you?"

"No. We've a God in Three Persons? Father, Son, and *ruach Hakodesh.* I think of Adonai the Father as male, Yeshua the Son, also as male, but I think of *ruach Hakodesh* as female. In fact, I believe that Adonai before anything was created, begat for Himself a nuclear family, and made them male and female. After all, Adonai said,

'Let us make humankind in our image, in the likeness of ourselves. So God created humankind in his own image; in the image of God he created them: male and female he created them.'"

"It's not exactly orthodox belief."

"No, but to me it makes sense. The word in Hebrew for the Holy Spirit is female in gender. It was the fecundity of the *ruach Hakodesh* that moved upon the waters to give birth to creation, and it was the *ruach Hakodesh* that begot Yeshua, and conceived Him in the womb of Mary before she produced any human ova. This I believe. And, who better for Yeshua to send to comfort us, to guide us in all truth and wisdom, and remind us of His word, but the *ruach Hakodesh*?"

"It might be so. Is tomorrow your Sabbath?"

"It is."

"Will you be going to your meeting house?"

"No. My being there might prove dangerous for my brothers and sisters."

"Steven will expect you to work with him tomorrow."

"And so I shall. I'll take my day of rest on Sunday, and if you permit, I'd like to go to church wih you."

"I'd like that."

Arms around one another we walk back to the house.

46

The rulings of Adonai are true, they are righteous altogether, more desirable than gold, than much fine gold, also sweeter than honey or drippings from the honeycomb. Through them your servant is warned; in obeying them there is great reward.

I kneel praying, and imagine myself a servant coming before my master, Adonai, being asked what I want.

Almighty and most merciful father, maker of all things You already know what I want. You know the situation that has arisen between Jean and myself. I ask that You would allow ruach Hakodesh to tell me Your will. In the name of Yeshua, Your Son I ask You this. I leave all in Your hands. Amen.

I get into bed. I think of Jean for a long time before falling asleep.
We meet at breakfast time.
"Sleep well, Stan?"
"Eventually Jean. You?"
"Eventually."
"Am I missing something?" Mary asks.
"Your detective, Gran, is courtin' my mum."
"Be good for them both."
"I was thinking, Stan, that today I'd have you working with the pigs, but you, being Jewish, and this being your Sabbath, I had second thoughts."
"I eat bacon and eggs, so why shouldn't I feed them? And the Sabbath was made for man not man for the Sabbath."
"You'll be doing more than feeding them, they need dunging out."
"Steven," Jean says, "that's not nice."
"You show me what to do and I'll dung them out."

I spend most of the morning making pigs comfortable, until 'Homecoming' and I am talking to Ima.

"Good Shabbat. For my son I have news."

"Good Shabbat Ima. You told Abba, that Yeshua is Messiah."

"I have, but about that later. What are you doing?"

"Feeding twenty pigs, and tending to a sow with a litter of twelve."

"Oy vey! swine already. A living prodigal, and on Shabbat. Where are you?"

"Can't say. There are people who want to know, and I do not want them to know."

"Already a man is asking, where is my son? Very rude man. Tell me his name he would not. I tell him I don't know because my son does not tell me."

"Such people you are working with. Are you in danger?"

"No, these pigs are quite friendly and the piglets are cute."

"*schmegegge!* I phone your friend, the Inspector, about this man. Told him what he looked like."

"So tell me."

She does. Tony Esposito.

"Tell me about Abba. How'd he take your good news?"

"Up his arms went, but your abba is allowing me to live in the same house with him until I come to my senses. Joanna says Abba knows on which side is buttered his bread."

"Did you tell Jo-Jo about your belief in Yeshua?"

"I did, everyone I tell. Trouble I ask for, my daughter says. To the synagogue I have not gone, because your abba said I should go with him, but the name of Yeshua I should not mention. To your synagogue I will go."

"You can go with Abba and sit behind the screen with the women and say the name of Yeshua."

"In your synagogue do women sit with men?"

"Meeting House, Ima. Men and women sit together. Just as when men and women sat together with Yeshua, when he walked on earth."

"Your mother will live with your father and I will come on Shabbat to your meeting house. Your father I will not leave, lonely, he would be."

"Good Shabbat Ima, my boss is coming."

"Good Shabbat, Stanley, for your mother, be careful."

"You finished?" Steven says.

"I am. The pigs look happier than you. Something you want to say."

"All right then, I'm not sure you should marry my mother."

"Have you told your mother that's the way you feel?"

"No. Are you going to ask her to marry you?"

"Already done."

"What did she say?"

"She said, 'yes'. Steven, speak to your mother, tell her how you feel; that you have a love and a concern for her; that you do not want to see her hurt; that your lives will be changed if she marries me."

47

"But why do you call Me 'Lord, Lord,' and not do the things which I say? Whoever comes to Me, and hears My sayings and does them, I will show you whom he is like: He is like a man building a house, who dug deep and laid the foundation on the rock. And when the flood arose, the stream beat vehemently against that house, and could not shake it, for it was founded on the rock. But he who heard and did nothing is like a man who built a house on the earth without a foundation, against which the stream beat vehemently; and immediately it fell. And the ruin of that house was great."

Jean and Mary have been busy. They've made an apple tart, wheaten farls, and scones. And for us workers, a lunch.

I say to Jean, "Will you walk with me this evening?"

"I will walk with you, Stan."

I take off for an afternoon along the river.

The river is two fields away, up one field and down the other to where there are stepping stones. I stay this side and walk along the bank following the flow.

On my way, I see a kingfisher taking fish. Further along I come to a large flat stone at the river bank. I sit and enjoy the sound of water over stones.

I turn my phone off. A quiet time. White clouds in the blue of the sky are zephyred lazily along towards the east of new beginnings.

I am there all afternoon, before becoming conscious of movement behind me. I turn quickly, half rising and I see four cows in a row standing watching me. When I rise, they follow me to the hedge I crossed coming into their field. I cross back and leave them staring at me over the hedge.

Later, after dinner, when I am walking with Jean, she laughs and tells me that cows have great curiosity.

"Jean," I say, "there are things about me I would like you to know."

"Stan, there is nothing about your past that I need to know."

"I was married before."

"I know, Mary told me, to a girl called Ruth. She also told me of what you said about a second marriage. I'm sure I'll like Ruth when the time comes to meet her, and I'm sure she would want you to love and cherish me, when we marry, as much as you did her."

"Well, *libling*, I cherish you now."

"Steven had a man to mother talk with me earlier."

"His mother is precious to him."

"He feels that you are too dangerous a man for me to marry."

"In a way he is right, for I'm putting all your lives in danger."

"You brought Mary here for safety."

"I did, and I still think she's safe."

"And you came here yourself for safety."

"No, I came here to be near you."

"I love you, Stan, and if we let God's word be a lamp to our feet and a light to our paths it is right for us to be together."

"You know your Psalms."

"We Presbyterians have the Scottish Metrical Psalter. That particular verse goes: *Thy word is to my feet a lamp and to my path a light, sworn have I, and I will perform, to keep Thy judgements right.*"

"Haven't heard it like that before. Do you sing psalms like that?"

"Sometimes, more often we get Townsend and Getty."

"Who are they?"

"Song writers, theologically sound, anything but poetic, and their music mostly un-memorable. You still coming with me tomorrow?"

"I am."

"Maybe we'll sing one of our psalms. Let's go back, I want to dance with you."

"In the house?"

"No, in the back yard."

Jean's not joking. We reach the back yard with its smooth concrete.

"We will dance here."

"We will? Without music?"

"The music will be in our heads. After we dance you tell me the tune in your head and I'll tell you the tune in mine."

She comes into my arms and we dance. The tune in my head waltzes her around and around. When we finish she says, "What was your tune?"

"The Blue Danube, but the song in my heart is you."

"Stan, you're a romantic."

"What was your tune?"

"The Tennesse Waltz. I was counting the beats."

"Jean, you're a pragmatic."

We kiss.

There is applause and we see Mary at the back door.

"You dance well together," Mary says.

We follow Mary inside to supper.

48

Next morning I'm introduced to Seamus MacCallion, and his son Eamon, who have been to early mass, and have come to allow us all to go off to Jean's Church.

This Sunday there should have been four of us going but Steven needs to stay to nurse a sick calf.

Mary and Jean get into my car.

"Tell me where to go, Jean," I say, driving out of the yard.

I drive as directed and we come to the church.

I park, and we get out.

"Your friends will be wondering who we are," Mary says.

"If I know anything, about our minister, Mr Williams, you'll soon be telling them," Jean says.

We enter, walk down the single isle and take our seats in a box pew on the right, Mary first, Jean, then myself.

On the dot of eleven, the robed minister enters the pulpit and the service begins with a welcome to all, especially those who are here for the first time. Mary and I are smiled upon.

"I have no doubt that our welcome would be more meaningful if we knew your names. Perhaps Jean you would introduce your friends."

"Of course, Mr Williams. The lady beside me is Mary Ford."

"We welcome you Mary," the minister says.

"Mary is Steven's grandmother."

"You have a fine grandson, Mary Ford. Jean and Steven have been part of our family here ever since she came home after the terrible loss of your son, and we hope that God has blessed you as he has blessed Jean. Shouldn't Steven be here?"

"He had to stay home to look after a sick calf," Jean says.

"And who is this other gentleman?"

"This is Stan, Stanley Eigerman. Stan, found me, and brought Mary to Steven and myself."

"Well now, I suppose sick calves need to be cared for. We welcome you Stanley." The man is astute.

"Thank you," I say.

"Perhaps Stanley you would tell us something about yourself. Are you a believer in Jesus Christ?"

"I know Him as Yeshua, the Messiah. Adonai, God, had Him call me from His Jewish race. I am also a private investigator."

"May I say something?" Mary asks.

"Yes, Mary."

"He is a very good at what he does. I asked him to find my son Steven's body and he did that. We're waiting confirmation that it's Steven."

"We may praise God and pray that is so. Perhaps you will join us after our service for a cup of tea?"

We stay after the service and people are friendly. While Jean and Mary talk with the women, I find myself with the men, until finally brought aside by Mr Williams, whose Christian name is Ralph.

We speak of the different manners in which Presbyterians and Messianic Jews praise and worship Adonai, Yeshua, and *ruach Hakodesh,* before he changes the subject.

"You know, Stanley, this is the first time I've seen Jean so animated. She seems to have lost a lot of her sorrow. She sorrowed a long time for Steven Ford."

I say nothing waiting for him to go on.

"Would I be right in thinking that this new found animation, happiness, is due to yourself?"

"I would say, Ralph, that you are right."

"And would I be right in thinking that you are as animated as she?"

"Again you are right. I am in love with Jean."

"And would I be right in thinking that is the reason Steven is not at church this morning."

"He is not sure that I should marry his mother."

"You intend to marry Jean?"

"I do, God willing. I like Steven and want to know him better."

"I must speak with Jean now."

We get back to the farm Steven says,

"Seamus and Eamon went early. I've been here by myself."

Jean says, "Mr Williams expects to see you at the evening service."

"Anything I can help you with today, Steven?" I ask.

"How much longer will you be with us?"

"Probably go back to Belfast late tomorrow."

"Then there's nothing I want you to do."

"I'm sure there's something Stan could do," Jean says, "while Mary and I prepare dinner."

"He could take a walk."

Later, Steven goes to church, and Jean, Mary and I enjoy each other's company.

49

Monday morning. 'Homecoming'.

"Ollie."

"Stanley. Bad or good? First or last?"

"Make it last."

"It's Steven's."

"Mazel tov."

"The guy who's been asking about your whereabouts is Tony Esposito."

"I'm coming back this afternoon, where will I see you?"

"Headquarters, I'll leave a pass for you at the gate. Just don't park in the Chief Constable's place."

"As if I would. See you, Ollie." Everyone looks at me expectantly. I put my phone away.

"Mary, you can stop putting fifty ps in that bottle. You'll be able to give Steven a proper Christian burial. Case closed."

"Stanley Eigerman, I love you," Mary gets up comes round the table, hugs me, bursts into tears. Sits again, and wipes her eyes on a small patch of cambric.

"Is the case really closed, Stan?" Jean says.

"Few loose ends, then we'll choose a ring. Mary, you'll stay with Jean and Steven, until I get things settled. I'd better pack my things."

"I'll give you a hand," Jean says. "I've washed and ironed your shirts and things."

In my room, I start packing. Jean hands me freshly laundred clothes.

"My dear, I wish you didn't have to go. You're safe here."

"Sooner or later, they'd find me here, and that will put you all in danger. I've got to go."

"It worries me."

"Jean, we're going to be together. Know what command is repeated most times in the Bible? *'Don't be afraid'*."

She puts her head on my chest and holds me tight. I feel her tremble.

"I'll try not to be."

I kiss her. Stroke her hair.

"Don't try, just obey the command."

"You don't understand, it's just…"

"I understand. You think that what happened to Steven will happen to me."

"I can't help thinking that. Let me go with you."

"You're needed here. Ollie and I will bring this to an end. Afterwards I'll no longer be in the P.I. business."

"What do you mean?"

"I mean I don't want you to be the wife of a private detective."

"Oh, Stan, be careful."

50

'Let the one who is doing harm continue to do harm; let the one who is vile continue to be vile; let the one who is righteous continue to live righteously; let the one who is holy continue to be holy.'

I get to that part of the road where I see Belfast lying in the valley between the hills and I realise how loath I am to leave the peace and quiet of the countryside.

At police headquarters I state my name, and I'm given a pass. The barrier is lifted and I drive on. I see the empty parking place for the Chief Constable. I overcome temptation.

I find Ollie in his office. No coffee. No doughnuts.

"Brass tacks, Stanley?"

"Brass tacks, Ollie."

"We're watching Esposito."

He's been sent to find me.

"Where is he now?"

"23, Slemish Street."

"Who else is there?"

"Bradley Martins. Armstrong's man."

"With a gun?"

"For certain."

"Ollie?"

"Yes, Stanley?"

"When all this is settled, will you be my best man?"

"I'm not circumcised."

"Nobody'll notice."

"You're serious?"

"Never more."

"Jean McBride?"

"Jean."

"We come out of this alive, certainly, I'll be your best man."

"Positive thinking. This is my last case."

"Glad to hear it. Your youth has fled."

"You put it so nicely."

"It's a gift I have. How about we go see Armstrong and Seymore tomorrow. I'll have Esposito and Martins brought in after we see their paymasters."

"It's a start."

***

We sit opposite Seymore and Armstrong.

"We hoped you were ghosts," Armstrong says.

"Dennis, I personally would like to see you repent of your sins and come over onto God's side."

"That's hokus pokus," says Seymore.

"Personally," says Ollie, "I'd let you rot for the hell you've created for others."

I say, "I'm going to testify against you, but I won't have to do that if…"

"They're offerin' us a deal, Larry," Dennie says.

"I was going to say, I wouldn't have to do that, if you make full confessions and plead guilty."

"We think it better if you two, and that auld doll, weren't around to testify."

"We'll be around."

"I wouldn't bet on it."

Laurence says, "We'll say no more."

"We're holding Esposito and Martins," Ollie says.

"Won't make an iota of difference," says Laurence.

"Nice word, iota."

"You'll still be dead meat," Dennie says.

"Dennis," I say, "please, do the right thing. You don't want to face God's judgement the way you are."

"Why should I repent? There ain't no judgement 'cos there ain't no God."

"Hokus pokus," says Seymore.

***

Another interview room. Tape whirling.

"Hallo, Tony."

"You could have killed me with them exhaust fumes."

"Naw, I knew what I was doin'. Good to see you fully recovered. You should get out of this kind of employment."

"You got nothing to arrest us for," Bradley says.

"You're not under arrest."

"Then what are we doin' here?"

"Chatting pleasantly."

"You talked to my family, Tony."

"Nice family, you need to take care of them. I fancy your sister."

"Well, you don't have to bother them any longer, you've found me."

"Can we go? We don't feel like chattin'," Bradley says.

"One of you is going to kill us. Which of you is going to pull the trigger?" I say.

"Me," says Tony, "I'll enjoy it. Then I'll go see your sister."

"Change sides, Tony. Come and be on the side of law and order."

"After what you done? I'll get you, even if…"

"Shut up! You talk too much, Tony," Bradley says.

"Can we go now?"

"You can go," says Ollie. "We'll keep an eye on you."

"Keep as many as you like."

Bradley stands, Ollie says, "I'll show you out."

When Ollie comes back I say, "If it's them, they couldn't care less about us knowing."

"Interesting how Bradley stopped Tony when he said: 'even if'."

"Which suggests?"

"That Tony is not the shooter, if it is shooting."

"Bradley?"

"Maybe, maybe not."

"Did we miss something? Pity we didn't tape it."

"I've got it on my phone."

We listen.

"Know what I think, Ollie?"

"I do, Stanley."

"There's a third man."

"It ain't Harry Lime. Let's hear what Seymore and Armstrong said."

"That's a devious phone you have, Ollie."

We listen.

"Well, well. Not Esposito, not Martins."

"Jo-Jo needs a bodyguard,Ollie. I think Tony intends to try for me before the third man."

"Might be right about Tony. We'll look out for your sister."

51

Who can say something and have it happen without Adonai's commanding it? Don't both bad things and good proceed from the mouth of the Most High.

I park in Slemish Street and knock on the door of 23, which is opened by Bradley.
"Tony in?"
"He's out."
"I want to talk with him."
"He wants to kill you."
"I'll try to disuade him."
"He won't listen. You took your life in your hands coming here."
"My life is in other hands."
"I heard about you. You don't pack a gun and you have invisible backup."
"Better believe it."
"Want to wait until he comes back? I wouldn't mind seing what happens."
"If it's no bother."
"No bother at all. Just one thing."
"What's that?"
"Don't talk about my immortal soul."
"Won't promise."
"I know, too much to ask."
When I'm in and sitting down:
"Just you and Tony here together."
"Yeah."
"Who cooks?"
"Tony."
"Italian?"
"Yeah."
"All that pasta."

"You can say that again."

"All that pasta."

"I didn't mean…"

"Couldn't resist it. What do you do? Send out for fish and chips?"

"KFC, or a Whopper."

"Why're you here with Tony?"

"Talk about my immortal soul if you want to."

"You won't listen."

"You're right."

"Whose house is this? It's not yours and it's not Tony's."

"Never you mind." His phone plays 'Black Knight'.

"What?" He listens. "OK, see you soon."

"That was Tony. Pretty soon you'll get a call."

"He doesn't know my number."

"Think not? He's on his way here."

"Good. I need to talk to him about the error of his ways."

"You're both in for a surprise."

Five minutes pass, and my phone plays 'Homecoming'.

"Hallo?"

"Eigerman."

"Tony."

"I got your sister."

"Prove it."

"Here, speak to your brother."

"Stan. Who is this man?"

"He's Tony Esposito."

"Believe me now? If you want her, you'll do like I say. I'll let you know later." He cuts off.

Bradley sits smiling broadly, in fact, he laughs.

"He's bringing your sister here, and he thinks you're somewhere else."

"Simplifies matters all round."

"Quite a coincience. Be interesting to see what happens."

"For every event there are always two wills at play. Tony's will is to get at me through my sister, and Adonai's will is bringing Tony and my sister to me. There are no coincidences."

"Two wills? What are you talking about. And who's Adonai?"

"Adonai, is God, Bradley. Let me tell you about the worst thing that ever happened that involved two wills."

"Which was what?"

"Heard of Jesus?"

"You'd have to be deaf, dumb, blind and not able to fight, in Northern Ireland, not to've."

"It was the will of that generation of Jewish and Roman authorities to crucify Jesus; it was Adonai's will that His Son should be crucified. Two wills. The Jews and the Romans meant it for their own evil purposes. Adonai, meant it for the good of the rest of his human creation."

"If God was responsible for all that, and everything else that happens, then we're puppets without free will."

"You have a God-given free will, for the use of which you are responsible. You know what to do for good, and what to do for evil, therefore you are held responsible for the choices you make, and you have to accept the consequences."

A key turns and a door opens.

52

Every kingdom divided against itself will be ruined, and every city or household divided against itself will not survive.

"Are you about?" Tony's call.

"In here." Bradley's answer.

"Come and give me a hand with this dame."

"You can manage yourself."

The door is pushed open.

"Get in there, you." Joanna is shoved into the room. Tony follows.

"What the…" When he sees me.

"Why Tony, how good of you to bring me my sister, safe and sound."

"What're you doin' here?"

"Waiting for you. We need to talk."

"You bring him here?" to Bradley.

"No, came on his own two feet."

"Why?"

"I think he wants to save your soul, pointin' out the error of your ways."

Tony pushes Joanna into a chair. "Sit, and don't move." He produces a gun.

"Tony, let my sister go."

"No way! Know what I'm gonna do with her?"

"That would be a sin, Tony. Not good."

"She'll enjoy it. But first I'm going to kill you."

"That would also be a sin, Tony."

Tony raises the gun.

A yell from Joanna. "You're a beast." She rises from the chair. Tony pushes her back.

"Say good-bye to your brother."

"Tony, put the gun down." Bradley, too has a gun.

"We want him alive."

"I want him dead." His finger whitening on the trigger.

Bradley shoots him. Tony goes down, dropping the gun. Bradley kicks it away.

"What'd you do that for?"

"We want you alive to testify against Seymore and Denny."

"Why?"

"We want everything Seymore has, and we want them convicted. Tony killed my uncle Sammy, on Dennie's say so."

Bradley puts away his gun. I went to Tony. No pulse. "He's dead."

"Phone your friend, Black."

"I won't lie about you."

"Don't expect anything else. I'll be leavin' now."

"Who's the third man?" I say.

"Don't know. I was to keep Tony from killin' you."

Bradley leaves. Joanna looks at Tony and shivers.

"He was awful, but when you see him like that…" another shiver.

I phone Ollie, and he tries to tell me he can't find Joanna.

"She's here with me." I tell him what has happened and he says he's on his way.

"I'll take you home, Jo-Jo, after I've made a statement to Ollie."

Ollie and the police ambulance arrive, and Tony's body is taken away.

Ollie records my statement on his phone. Puts the gun in an evidence bag.

"I've put out an alert for Martins," Ollie says.

"Has this brother of yours Joanna, asked about your welfare?"

"He's been far too busy searching this place, for what I don't know."

"Well, I'll take you home and you'll have dinner with Hanna, and myself, after which you can tell me all about how you came to be here. You should be ashamed of yourself, Stanley."

"Yes, Ollie."

I drive home.

"*Adonai*," I say as I'm heating tomato soup.

"*Thank you for your will in all that happened this day. For the deliverance of Jo-Jo. You know my heart was trembling the whole time. You know I love her, but was at a loss what to say to her afterwards. Thank you for Ollie. Thank you that your Spirit prevailed and your will was done. I'm only sorry about Tony.*"

I make tea, bring bread, get a spoon, pour my soup into a bowl, take it to the table, sit down and say:

"Adonai, sometimes I think that even if pity is shown to those who are wicked like Tony, they don't learn what righteousness is. They sin, and fail to see Your Majesty. I know that where You are, Lord Yeshua, you are praying for me, but please, pray for Paul, Ifeta, Bradley, Thomas and William as well as this third man, that they too will come to be with you when you make all things new. Bless this food and give me strength to glorify your Father, Adonai. Amen."

After I eat, I let Mahler's fourth symphony take me through the emotions of the day.

53

In the morning, I phone Jean. I want to hear her voice, and tell her I love her. I ask how Mary is, and Steven. She tells me they are both getting on like a house on fire.

"Stan, how are things with you?"

"Ollie and I have been tying up loose ends, and we think there is just one more, and then I'll retire."

"Have you thought of what you might do?"

"A little."

"Tell me."

"After this last loose end is tied up."

"Some inkling?"

"Not one."

"Beast! Is this loose end going to be difficult and dangerous?"

"It may be difficult."

"And dangerous?"

"Somewhat."

"But you'll have Ollie."

"I'll have Ollie."

"I love you, Stan."

"And I love you, Jean. Fear not."

After, I phone Jo-Jo.

"Jo-Jo, what can I say? Are you all right?"

"After such an ordeal, I should be all right."

"You sound like Ima."

"What if I do? The way he touched me! I could have killed him."

"You were saved from that, thankfully. You must have been shocked to see him killed."

"By that other awful man."

"Want to talk about it?"

"I'm O.K. I talked it over with Ollie."

"Good to have such a friend. Joanna, I'm sorry for what happened to you. I'm sorry I wasn't more comfort to you."

"It's all right. I heard you asking about a third man. Is that why you were searching that house?"

"For a clue to who he is and where he might be."

"Take care, Stan."

"Care I will take, sister mine, so that you will come to my wedding. Adonai bless you."

"Your wedding? What do you mean?"

"Later." I smile as I break the connection. My phone plays immediately.

"What this about your wedding?"

"I'm in love with a girl called Jean, who is in love with me, and whose eyes are green."

"Tell me more."

"Got to go."

"Don't you dare go."

I dared, and cut the power to my phone. I power up again, when I get to my office. 'Homecoming' again.

"Stanley, this is your Ima. About your wedding I am not to be told? My son talks to his sister before he talks to his Ima. When takes place this wedding? A nice Jewish girl you found for yourself?"

"Her name is Jean, a Messianic Gentile. You'll like her."

"Can this Jean make for me a grandchild?"

"When I marry Jean you will already be a *Bubbeh*. His name is Steven, he's twenty-one. Mary's grandson."

"Oi. Oi. Oi! Another family I have already."

"All true children of Abraham."

"To tell your abba, a grandfather he is to be, in this way, what words will I hear!"

"Ima, there's a few things I have to do, but when they're done, I'll take you to see Jean."

"Maybe your abba will be included."

"If he will come."

"Your Ima will see that your abba will come."

"Until then, Ima."

"Mazel Tov, Stanley."

What I need, I say to myself is a few black bags and some banana boxes, as I eye my office which I am closing down. I'll aslo need a shredder. Phone yet again.

"Ollie."

"Stanley. How about we have a day off? Go fishing."

"You have something in mind."

"Nine in the morning. Go get your gear together."

54

"Ollie, this fishing lodge, you're taking me to seems pretty remote."

"Very remote."

"Trout, Salmon, or something bigger? We're being followed."

"Of course we are."

"Should we try to lose them."

"We're the bait on this fishing trip."

"You got backup at the lake, Ollie?"

"A few stout-hearted men, Stanley."

"And if he has a rifle?"

"Always a possibility."

"Try not to kill him, Ollie."

"May not work out that way."

"Let's try to take him alive."

"We can but try."

We make a turn to the right and cross a bridge over a wide river. The other car pulls up before the turn. Two miles on, we come to the fishing lodge.

We walk in and show our permits and licences to the man behind the bar. There are four other fishermen, sitting, talking again after seeing us. Stout hearted men.

"Many on the river today?" Ollie asks.

"A good number," the man replies. "What are you after?"

"Salmon. What's the water like?"

"Water's clear and less deep now than it was. What were you thinkin' of usin'?"

"Ally's Shrimp."

"Good for all types of water any time of year. What about you?" he asks me.

"What are they takin'?"

"Man out there now, swears by the Stoat's Tail."

"I got that," I say, and would have said more except the door through which we entered opens and a sharp faced woman enters and calls loudly, "Eigerman! Black!" We turn, she has a gun in her hand. Ollie reaches for his, and hers moves to shoot him. I throw myself between her and Ollie, and hear the crack of her pistol. After that, nothing.

55

I may speak in the tongues of men, even angels; but if I lack love, I have become merely blaring brass or a cymbal clanging.

Voices coming from right of me.

"When you remove the bullet will he be all right, Doctor?" *Abba's voice.*

When I try to turn to see him I cannot. I am conscious, aware but cannot move a muscle.

"There is a good chance he will be." *That must be the doctor.*

I try to speak. I want to say, "What's the matter with me?" but I can't.

"Doctor!" *an exclaimation from my Ima.* "His eyes moved, he's blinking."

Yes, I can move my eyes and lids.

The doctor shines light into my eyes. "A good sign, I would say he is fully conscious. Move your right arm."

I can't. He uncovers my feet and scrapes my soles. No movement.

He comes so that I can see his face.

"Do you understand what I say. Two blinks for yes, one for no."

I blink twice.

"Right, good. I'm your surgeon, Robert Hanna. A neuro-surgeon, and I am going to operate on your brain because there is a bullet I must remove. Got all that?"

"Two blinks."

"At the moment, all that part of your nervous system which normally causes movement and speech has been paralysed. On the other hand that part of your nervous system which allows you to move your eyes and lids and experience sensations is still functional. Also, your thinking is functional, and that is a good sign. You have what is known as Locked in Syndrome. Understand?"

Two blinks. He's smiling at me.

"Good man. Now, I believe, when I remove the bullet which is affecting your brain stem and holding you captive, there is a 50-50 chance you will regain your ability to move, and of course to talk. Your father has given permission for me to operate, but now that you are conscious and can understand, do you give permission also?"

Two blinks.

"Very well, I'll leave you with your parents."

"So he can see better, can my son sit up?" Ima says.

"I'll get the nurse to adjust the bed." He goes out.

"We will talk with you like the doctor," Ima looks into my face. "What is it with my son getting shot?"

"He can only blink 'yes' or 'no'," Abba says.

A nurse comes in and pumps up the bed so I am lying semi-upright. I close my eyes and my body begins to float towards the wall I see opposite. When I open my eyes I'm where I was. Ima and Abba are at the foot of the bed where I can see them without moving my head.

"Can you see us?"

Two blinks. They look at each other. Will they tell me what I want to know?

Adonai, I want to know: Is Ollie all right? Did the woman shoot Ollie? Where's Jean? Does she know what's happened to me?

"Joanna is now disengaged from the atheist," Abba says.

"My son needs not to know that now. That is something for later."

"My daughter is the one keeping the faith of our ancestors. This is what you and your son get for following a cult."

"Nathan Eigerman! What a thing to say! What you have become, a Pharisee, more than Stanley, you love more your old Law. Be ashamed! Stanley can hear every thoughtless word you say."

"Good, I want him to hear. When the doctor says he has a 50-50 chance of survival after this operation, he probably meant his chances were less. I want him on the side of Adonai's Law."

"I will pray to Yeshua, that my son survives."

"He'll need to give you a miracle if he survives with all his faculties, and is able to walk and talk."

"Then a miracle he will have."

As the surgeon had done Abba, comes closer to me, "Do you renounce this Yeshu as a false prophet?"

One blink.

"Say yes!"

One blink.

"You will die divorced from the covenant given to Moses by Adonai, if you do not deny this false prophet that says he is the Son of God."

I close my eyes.

"Now look what you've done." *I hear Ima say.* "Nathan Eigerman, take yourself home. Damage you have done enough. Go! Another word from you, we do not want to hear."

"You too, are in error with this, Yeshu."

"Enough already. Go!"

"How will you get home?"

"Go! Here I stay."

"Don't be unreasonable."

"Ashamed you should be."

The door opens and closes. I open my eyes. Ima is where I can see her.

"Do you hear me, Stanley?"

Two blinks.

"You must forgive your father. He means well, but wrong he is about everything."

Two blinks.

"When this bullet is removed, and on your own two feet you are standing, he will see how wrong he is. I will go now for Nathan will be waiting for me in the corridor."

Ima kisses me.

56

I've been asleep. I don't know for how long. As I become conscious someone is lifting my arm then letting it fall. I turn my head. *I turn my head!* I see a nurse.

"What are you doing?" I say. *I'm talking!*

"Checking for movement."

"What's happened?"

"You've had your operation."

The nurse brings me a mirror. I see my bandaged head.

"It's called a capeline bandage. We're all very pleased."

Another nurse comes and they change my position.

"Mr Hanna will be in to see you."

"I'm no longer locked in."

"Great, isn't it?"

"Will I be allowed visitors?"

"In time. We're all very pleased Mr Eigerman. Press the buzzer if you need anything." They smile and depart.

Being locked in is not something I'd want to happen again, to me, or to anyone else.

Is Ollie alive or dead? Is the woman alive or dead? Does Jean and Mary know what happened to me? Are they safe? Is there someone else out there waiting to kill me? Has Mary buried Steven?

Mr Hanna comes in.

"Well, Mr Eigerman, How are you?"

"I can move and talk."

"Excellent." He looks at my charts. "Let me tell you what happens next. You're going to be here a while, because your strength needs to build up, so you will be seeing the dietician and you will be going to physiotherapy where they will teach to stand and walk again."

"Surely I know how to stand and walk."

"It's not as easy as talking. Your bladder tone will need restoring after we take your catheter out."

"If this was a detective story, I'd be up and about detecting in full vigour."

"Unfortunately when real life detectives get head injuries and survive, they need a change of employment. From now on, you must avoid being hit anywhere on the head."

"Was it a difficult operation?"

"It was."

"Then you're very good."

"My mother tells me I'm a genius, and your mother tells me you're a Messianic Jew. All I can say is, that I believe that I had help from your Jehovah."

"We call Him Adonai, and His Son, Yeshua. When will I be allowed visitors?"

"Let's give it a few days more. I'll keep your mother and father informed and let them know when they can see you."

"Will you do something for me."

"What is it?"

"I'll give you a number, and will you ring Inspector Black."

"Inspector Black has been asking about you."

"So, Ollie's alive. That's one thing I wanted to know. Did he kill the woman who shot me?"

"She's in custody."

"Thank Yeshua for that."

"Anything else, Mr Eigerman?"

"No. Stan, call me Stan. I am grateful to you for my release. Has there been anybody else asking for me?"

"Yes, Stan, Jean McBride, and Mary Ford have been most concerned and insistent upon knowing about you throughout your locked in period, and before and after your operation. I assured them you'll make a full recovery."

"All that puts my mind at rest."

"Ah, the mind. Yes, an entirely different entity than that grey and white mass of cells I operated on. Now, I must go."

I won't go into detail about how I learned to sit up without flopping, how I learned to transfer from bed to wheelchair, or how I learned to stand, and then walk, or how my bladder returned to normal. The fact is *Adonai, Yeshua,* and *ruach Hakodesh* gave me good physio and occupational therapists.

I had visitors who took me in a wheelchair to the hospital canteen. The first, was Ollie.

"Stanley."

"Ollie."

"You took a bullet for me."

"I did, I have it here, .22, do you want it?"

"Of course. The best way to get a bullet."

I took from my dressing gown pocket what Robert Hanna had taken from my head and gave it to Ollie.

"Thanks Stanley, not for the bullet, but for my life. I owe you."

"I need no return on that, Ollie. Anyway, my detecting days are over. I can no longer afford to be hit on the head. Who would hire a detective with a crash helmet on his head? Now, tell me, who was that lady who shot me."

"Lucrezia Clemento. Hard as nails."

"Glad you didn't kill her."

"Wounded."

"What about Seymore and Armstrong?"

"Armstrong's dead. Killed in prison. Seymore's in protective confinement. Thinks the same will happen to him."

"When's his trial?"

"April."

"April is the cruelest month. I'm leaving the wasteland, Ollie, to you."

"While you do what?"

"Get married for a start."

"Always a good start."

"Has Mary been given Steven's remains?"

"Not yet, but soon." His phone rang. "The wasteland calls."

57

Today I get out. Dressed, I wait for Jean who is coming to collect me and take me to the farm. I wait, thinking over the conversations I had during this past time with my visitors.

Mary came, feeling guilty; felt it was her fault what happened to me.

"No need to feel that way, Mary."

"But, if I hadn't…"

"You did me a favour."

"A favour?"

"I'm going to be step-father to your grandson?"

"Ach…"

"And is that not good fortune?"

"What about your profession? I'm told…"

"I am no longer a professing detective."

"What will you do? I owe you for what you've done."

"All those fifty p's?"

"You must take more than that?"

"I'm not even going to take the fifty p's."

"You have to take something."

"Your friendship, Mary. I'll take your friendship."

"You have that already. You and Jean."

"Good. You are now my goyish mama."

"Does that give me privileges?"

"You can tell me when to change my socks, and knit me woolen pullovers."

"They've given me Steven's remains. There's room in his father's grave. Will you be able to come to his funeral?"

"I'll be there."

"Thank you, Stan, for finding him. I'm just sorry you had to suffer."

"The suffering was a pleasure, and all mine."

"What does an unemployed detective do?"

"I have a police pension, savings, and something in mind."

"Something you've talked over with Jean?"

"Not yet."

"Then I'll not ask what it is until you do."

Steven came.

"Good to see you on your feet, Stan."

"Best feeling in the world. How's the farm."

"Pigs were askin' for you. Not too happy without you."

"I'll renew my acquaintance with them when Jean brings me home. Tell me the truth, Steve, I'm going to be your stepfather, you happy with that?"

"The truth. Well…You goin' to be close to her now you're no longer detectin'?"

"I am."

"Mum's happy, but I'll be lookin' out for the way you're lookin' after her."

"I wouldn't expect less. You're wondering where we'll live when we marry."

"Where are you going to live?"

"It won't be on the farm. We'll buy a place of our own."

"Where?"

"Where Jean and I decide. The farm is yours. You'll need help with it. I know someone who might help you out. His name is Paul. He's big, and he's strong. Make a good farm labourer. Stay a while he'll be here."

"Has he ever worked on a farm?"

"No, but he'll learn."

"I don't know…What's his background?"

"I'd rather he told you."

When Paul arrived, first thing he said was,

"They tell me you're gettin' out. You'll need a bodyguard."

"I'm getting out, Paul, but no bodyguard. This is Steve. He's in need of someone to help him, I thought of you. Steve this is Paul."

"Hi, Paul."

"Hi, Steve. You need a bodyguard?"

"No…I…"

"I'd better explain, Paul, Steve's and his mother live on a farm. I'm going to marry his mother…"

"You are?"

"I am, so he won't have her help around the farm anymore. He needs a good farm hand. Would you be willing?"

"What's a farm hand do?"

"Gets up early and goes to bed late."

"And in between?"

"Works very hard."

"What's the pay?"

"Steve?"

"It's more than the minimum wage."

"That's what I'm getting now. How much more."

"Ten percent more. You'll be well fed, and you'll have a bed."

"Stan, you want me to do this?"

"I thought you might like to help Steve out. Your decision."

"This might be good for the problem I have."

"What problem?"

"You know who's been tryin' to get me to come back. Kinda forcing me, and I don't want to."

"You thinking if you move to the country, they won't know where you are?"

"That's about it. I don't know if Steve'll want me. You tell him anything about me?"

"Nothing."

"He should know."

"So tell him."

And he did in all truth. When he finished, no one said anything until Steve spoke, "Right, Paul, we'll help each other. Know anything about farm work?"

"No, been a townie all my life, but you show me what you want done, and how to do it, and I'll do it. I'm good with engines."

58

May the words of my mouth and the thoughts of my heart be acceptable in your presence, Adonai, my rock and redeemer.

Ima, of course was a constant visitor. We spoke of many things, of love and of her approval of Jean, laughing when I told her that Mary had become my goyish mama, and her goyish sister.

Abba came to see me.

"Abba."

"Stanley."

"Good you have come. If you hadn't, I would have come to you after I got out, for I remember our last meeting when the words of your mouth and the thoughts of your heart were hurtful to me, and for which I forgive you. Your words that day were not acceptable. What righteous father bullies his son the way you did?"

"You dishonour me with this Yeshu."

"Yeshua. I respect and honour you for bringing me through my childhood and boyhood in the precepts of the Old Covenant, but unlike you, still waiting for a messiah, I found the Messiah, Yeshua, through whom Adonai made his New Covenant of faith so that nobody could boast of having saved themselves by adhering to laws impossible to keep. If you feel I have dishonoured you because of that I am sorry, but I will not recant."

"I will not recant from Adonai's Covenant with Moses."

"Perhaps."

"I think not. Your mother has left me. If you had not given her that *B'rit Hadashah* she would not have left me."

"Ima has not left you, Abba, nor have I. We have only left the synagogue of the Old Covenant, because we know that the Old Covenant given to Moses, is fulfilled by Yeshua, our Messiah."

"Adonai is one and we Jews are His children through Abraham."

"True enough, we are physically descended from Abraham, but we must also be faithfully descended, for it was through his faith that Abraham was accepted by Adonai before he was circumcised, and before the Law was given to Moses."

"We are Jews, chosen people, we do not need this Christian gospel you preach."

"Adonai preached the gospel of Yeshua, to Abraham, saying, *'In you shall all the nations be blessed.'* There are not two peoples of God, through two different identities, Jews and Christians. These two identities become irrelevant, when they become one entity through faith in Yeshua. When the circumcised Jew and the uncircumcised Gentile have faith in Yeshua, Abraham is their father and they are his true sons and daughters."

"Stop! Stop this conversation."

"Very well. Let us agree to differ. You with the *Tanakh* and me with *B'rit Hadashah.*"

"I hear you're getting married."

"Nothing wrong with your hearing."

"To a Shiksa."

"To a Messianic Gentile woman. Her name is Jean. Will you come to our wedding?"

"Remains to be seen."

"Ima likes her."

"Then I'll be at your wedding. When and where will it be?"

"After April. Late *Iyyar* or early *Sivan* ~ Maytime. The location at the moment is known only to my rabbi and Jean's minister."

"Your mother doesn't know?"

"Not yet."

"Ha!"

"Has this woman…"

"Jean."

"Has Jean sisters or cousins for bridesmaids?"

"None, but she has three bridesmaids, one called Mary, another Joanna."

"Our Joanna?"

"My sister. Jean will be given to me by her son, Steven. Her father and mother are no longer earthbound."

"Our Joanna! And that's another thing. Your mother has got Joanna to put on her phone the *B'rit Hadashah.*"

"I hope she reads it."

"What has my family come to? This boy, this Jew, I brought into the world is to marry a Shiksa, who has a son already, who is to give her away. And my wife who lives with me, but who has departed from me, is luring away my daughter who is to be a bridesmaid at what kind of wedding?"

"Abba. It will be the kind of wedding Yeshua enjoyed at Cana."

"You intend to have water turned into wine?"

"Not at all, Abba. We give you wine which your kidneys will turn into water."

"All right. All right. Your mother doesn't have to tell me to come to your wedding, This wedding I must see."

"Come with your blessing."

"The blessing I come with will be for the son of my loins. I will not give my blessing to his beliefs."

"Yeshua, Jean, and myself accept your coming with such a blessing. Ifeta Bozić will also be there with Joshua Horowitz."

"That atheist! Ifeta Bozic, who is this?"

"The third bridesmaid. The girl you examined when I brought her to you from the brothel. You'll meet her again at my wedding."

59

Just before Jean arrives I get a call from Ollie.

"New developments, Stanley."

"Do tell, Ollie."

"Seymore has made a deal with the Niffties, and is back communing with the rest of the prisoners. Not a hair on his head is to be touched."

"Big deal?"

"All his worldly goods signed over to the Niffty overlords in return for his life."

"Including his money?"

"Remains with his wife."

"He trusts her?"

"Take it to be so. She doesn't like us."

"You think?"

"En garde, encore. There may be another Clemento."

"Got to go, Jean's just arrived."

"My regards."

"So long." I close my phone. "Right on time, my dear. That was Ollie, he sends his regards."

"How nice." Jean is followed by a nurse with a wheelchair.

"What's that for?"

Nurse: "I will wheel you to the front door."

"I can walk."

"You will be wheeled. It's policy."

"I will be wheeled. You brought what we decided on, Jean?"

"Left at the desk for everyone."

"A feast of traybakes," says the nurse. "We thank you."

I am wheeled to the front door, passing everyone, thanking them, saying goodbye. At the door, I say farewell to the wheelchair.

"And now, Jean my love, dance me home."

"Quick step or waltz?"

"Waltz, three-four time is romantic."

We make the journey to the farm in her Land Rover.

"Jean, I'd like to think that this last case of mine was finished, but it may not be." I tell her what Ollie said about Seymore and his wife, and there may be another Clemento.

"So, I think I'd be putting you and Steven in danger if I stay at the farm."

"You'll be safe at the farm with us."

"I still think…"

"Stop thinking. We'll look after you. By the way, Mary is holding Steven's funeral on Thursday. I'm going to fatten you up a bit more."

"I'm in good trim."

"You're a bit slim. Mr Hanna says you need to build up your strength. So, a good sleep tonight and a big breakfast in the morning."

"How's Paul doing?"

"Steven's pleased to have him, and Paul's happy at his work. He'll tell you himself."

"Good to hear. But I still need this case to finish."

"But first, I'm going to see to your convalescence."

Next morning I wake up at 10am. I come to the kitchen, nobody is there.

I find Paul, with the pigs.

"How's it going, Paul?"

"I like it. Good job."

"Seen Jean this morning?"

"Gone to town."

"Know what for?"

"To see Selma."

"Selma Seymore. She doesn't know where she lives."

"She asked me, I told her."

My heart sinks. *Adonai, Yeshua, Ruach Hakodesh, be merciful and keep Jean safe.*

I phone Ollie.

60

Selma Seymore lived in a million pound mansion in a private mews off the Malone Road.

Jean parked the Land Rover and mounted four steps to the front door. She rang the bell and waited. The door opened.

"Mrs Seymore?" asked Jean.

"Yes, I'm Mrs Seymore." Selma Seymore had a very polite way of pronouncing her words. "And what may I do for you, my dear?"

"I've come about Stanley Eigerman."

"What about him?" The polite pronounciation evaporated.

"May I come in?"

"Who are you anyway?"

"I'm Jean McBride."

"If you're a friend of Eigerman's you're not welcome."

"Is Stanley Eigerman's life in danger? Your husband wants him dead. Has he hired someone, through you, to kill him?"

"Bring her in," said a man's voice.

Jean's arm is taken and she is dragged through the doorway. The door is closed and she finds herself in a hall with packed suitcases. Selma brings Jean into a room with curtains closed over the windows. The man turns on the light.

"Now, Jean McBride, tell me what makes you think Selma's husband has put a contract on Eigerman through her?"

"It wouldn't be the first time."

"No, it wouldn't."

"Who are you?"

"The invisible man."

"Well, has he? Stan put her husband where he is, and will testify against him. She's his wife, he put all the money in her name, and he expects her to use part of it to hire someone to kill Stan."

"You know a lot, but not all his money is in my name," Selma said. "He's money in Geneva. I got what was in banks here. I've no intention of wasting it hiring, hit men. As far as I'm concerned Larry Seymore can rot in jail. He gave away everything to save his miserable hide, and left me without a roof over my head. We're packed and ready to go. Right, Brad?"

"What's your interest in Eigerman, anyway?" Brad asked.

"I'm going to marry him."

"Fancy that!"Selma said, "I'm getting rid of a husband, and you're taking one on. Good luck with that."

"Do you not love your husband? Surely you should stand by him."

"We'll be long gone when he's banged up."

"You took vows when you married?"

"Ach, everybody takes them. They don't mean a thing."

"They mean commitment."

"I'm committed. To my happiness and prosperity."

"At least your honest about it. You must have loved your husband at one time."

"I loved what he gave me. Now I know he's going down for murder he's no use to me. All the hotels and houses. All gone. At least, I have some of his money."

"The money means more than your husband?"

"You bet it does."

"It won't last."

"Niether did he."

"Your Judgement day will come"

"Let us know when," said Brad.

"Last minute repentance might be right but if it for the wrong reason…"

"I have no intention of bendin' the knee to God."

"You're a hard man "

"That I am."

"You'll find God a harder man than you. I've seen you somewhere before."

"You think?"

"Yes. Stan is safe?"

"He's safe as far as we're concerned."

"Then I'll go."

"No you won't."

"What do you mean?"

"You've remembered who I am. And you know my name."

"Bradley Martins. The police are looking for you."

"They are indeed, so you can't go."

"You should let me leave."

"No chance."

"You're being foolish."

"Bring some of that duck tape."

Selma brought duck tape. Jean did not resist the tapeing of her hands and feet and her body to a straight-backed chair.

Selma takes Jean's car keys, goes out, and comes back shortly.

"Time to go, Brad," she said.

"Earlier than we thought, nevertheless."

They departed leaving Jean taped to the chair, breathing through her nose.

61

After I phone Ollie, I drive to Belfast and phone him again when I get there.

"Where are you?"

He speaks quietly. "In bushes outside Seymore's."

"What's happening?"

"Jean's Land Rover's sitting outside the front door."

"Any sign of Jean?"

"Inside."

"I'll be right there."

Takes ten minutes. I park behind Ollie's car and do what he probably did, walk up the drive under cover of trees and bushes. I join him.

"You sure Jean's in there? How long have you been here."

"She's in there all right. I got here before she did, saw her arrive. Selma let her in. Hasn't come out yet."

"Back door?"

"Got a man round the back. No one's come out."

"What are we waiting for? We need to go in." My anxiety is rising.

"Peace, and patience, Stanley."

"She's been in there too long." I start forward.

"Wait, door's opening."

It's not Jean who comes out, but Selma. She goes to the garage, drives her car out, leaves the engine running. She gets into Jean's Land Rover, drives it into the garage, closes the door, and goes back into the house.

"Come on, Ollie."

Just as we get near to the front door, Selma and Bradley Martins come out with cases.

"Bonnie and Clyde," says Ollie. "Hold it Martins!" Ollie has his gun aimed at Martins. He blows a whistle while I pass him and run inside.

"Jean! Jean, where are you?"

I keep calling and looking in places she isn't. I hear a bump, and find her in the chair she's toppled, trying to scrape along towards the door.

"Oh, Jean, Jean, Jean." I set the chair upright. I take hold of the tape across her mouth. "This will hurt, I'm sorry." I whip it off quickly.

"Selma and Bradley Martins…"

"We know. Ollie has them. They left you here trussed up like a turkey, you could have died." I free her from the chair.

"I was sure you'd find me."

"Thanks to Adonai. What did you hope to achieve coming to see Selma?"

"I wanted to make sure you'd be all right. She told me that she and Bradley Martins were off somewhere with her husband's money, and that she was not wasting a penny of what she got hiring a hit-man to kill you. That's why I came, and I'm glad I did."

I hear the siren of a police van arriving.

"Let's get you out of here."

We get to the door and see the handcuffed Selma and Bradley being placed in the van.

"Good to see you, Jean," Ollie says. "Do you think you could come down to headquarters and tell us all about your little adventure?"

After Jean made, and signed her statement, and Ollie and I are alone, I say, "Selma could be lying."

"Maybe, maybe not. Seymore and Armstrong have other friends. "

"Think the best, prepare for the worst. Something to eat is best."

Jean and I dine with Ollie, then we drive home, she in her Land Rover, I in my car. Steve and Paul want to know what happened.

"Tomorrow," Jean says. "I'd like to rest."

"Reaction setting in," I say.

So, while Jean rests, I say, "You are not to allow her to do anything like that again."

"Hardly likely," says Steve.

"I'll keep an eye out," says Paul.

The next evening I'm walking with Jean along the river bank.

"You did a full day's work today."

"Only way I know when I need to settle myself."

"Settled?"

"God is good. Were you angry with me?"

"Yes, I was. And with Steve and Paul."

"Did you sin?"

"I don't think so. I hope not. Were they rough with you?"

"Not really."

"No concern for yourself?"

"Some, but none after I heard your voice. You sounded in such a state."

"I was in such a state. I thought…"

"I know what you thought but there was no need to."

"There was every need to. Bradley killed Tony, and Selma's no angel. Look, Jean, don't go off on your own like that again. Promise?"

"Promise. Now that we know there's nobody out to kill you and Ollie."

"Still, we have to be vigilant."

"Is that why Paul is having an evening stroll a hundred yards behind us?"

"He's keeping an eye out."

"You think Selma lied to me."

"Best to think that. Seymore has other friends, so has Armstrong."

"I'm sure she didn't lie. And, by the way, what's a convalescent like you doing, dashing around saving damsels in distress?"

"They will put themselves in jeopardy."

"What will you do when this is all over?"

"What we will do. I've thought of something, but it will mean you leaving farming."

"I thought it might. In fact, I've already done something about that."

"You have?"

"Paul works well here on the farm, and Steve has a grudging liking for him, but they hate each other's cooking and neither knows how to keep the farm house clean, so it came to me that Steve's grandmother might like to come and do womanly stuff."

"You've asked Mary?"

"I have, and just as soon as Steve's remains are buried, she'll come and live here."

"Forward planning. What does Steve say?"

"He's in favour. Now, what have you got in mind for us?"

"Next year in Jerusalem."

62

So from now on, we do not look at anyone from a worldly viewpoint. Even if we once regarded the Messiah from a worldly viewpoint, we do so no longer. Therefore, if anyone is united with the Messiah, he is a new creation—the old has passed; look, what has come is fresh and new!

"Stanley, what do you think?"

"I think, Mary, that you should leave that to God."

"But, I doubt if either Steven or his father died in a state of grace."

"None of us can say for sure about another's spiritual state."

"I know, I know, but I can't help thinking of them in…in…in the wrong place."

"Mary, today we give Steven's remains a resting place. Up to now you grieved and worried because you didn't know where he was. Now, are you going to grieve and worry over this unknown?"

"But it's different. Where will Steven and Paddy spend eternity. They'll be in one place or the other."

"Mary my goyish mother, Yeshua, our Messiah, doesn't want you to be anxious about things you can do nothing about. He wants you to be immediate, and live to bring His Kingdom on earth, as it is in heaven."

"But I can't help thinking…"

"Give over. Give your mind to Yeshua. He will renew it, and give you peace. Through you, He wants to spread His love. Look who he's given you. Jean, a grandson, a Jewish son, through us He shows his love for you."

"You want me to give my head peace."

"Just be still, He'll show you that those are not thoughts you should have."

***

Steven's remains are brought to the graveside around which we are standing. Reverend Ralph Williams, Mary, Jean, Steven, Paul, Ollie, his wife, Hanna, Ima, Abba, myself, and Rabi Jacob Waldbaum from my congregation, attending as an act of *tzedakah*.

As Mr Williams conducted the church service, Rabbi Waldbaum reads at the graveside:

Look, I will tell you a secret—not all of us will die! But we will all be changed! It will take but a moment, the blink of an eye, at the final shofar. For the shofar will sound, and the dead will be raised to live forever, and we too will be changed. For this material which can decay must be clothed with imperishability, this which is mortal must be clothed with immortality. When what decays puts on imperishability and what is mortal puts on immortality, then this passage in the Tanakh will be fulfilled: "Death is swallowed up in victory. Death, where is your victory? Death, where is your sting?" The sting of death is sin; and sin draws its power from the Torah; but thanks be to God, who gives us the victory through our Lord Yeshua the messiah! So, my dear brothers and sisters, stand firm and immovable, always doing the Lord's work as vigorously as you can, knowing that united with the Lord your efforts are not in vain.

May the great name of Adonai be exalted and sanctified, throughout the world, which he has created according to his will. May His kingship be established in your lifetime and in your days, and in the lifetime of the entire household of Israel, swiftly and in the near future; Amen. May His great name be blessed, forever and ever. Blessed, praised, glorified, exalted, extolled, honoured, elevated and luaded be the name of the holy one, Blessed is he—above and beyond any blessings and hymns, praises and consolations which are uttered in the world; Amen. May there be abundant peace from Heaven, and life, upon us and upon all Israel; Amen.

That said, and with a final act of *tzedakah* I, Abba, and Rabbi Waldbaum fill in the grave over the mortal remains of Steven Ford. We do this because it is our obligation to obey Adonai's two greatest commandments: to love Adonai, with all our hearts, souls, minds and strength, and our neighbours as ourselves.

Back at the farm we all have a meal together.

Mary asks Rabbi Waldbaum, "Was that a Jewish prayer you prayed at the graveside?"

"It is a Jewish orthodox prayer, a doxology that glorifies the name of Adonai, Am I right, Nathan?"

Abba says, "It is used as the mourner's prayer. The Kaddish."

"Perhaps you would explain the purpose of the Kadish, Nathan."

"After the loss of a parent, in order that a son or daughter might not lose faith in Adonai, or to cry out about Him being unjust, Judaism requires the mourner to stand up every day, publicly, and re-affirm that Adonai is the Almighty One, despite this loss. In the eyes of Adonai, the deceased must have been very good to raise a child or relative who could express such faith in the face of personal loss."

"How long is the mourning period?" Jean asks.

"Twelve months."

"So the Kaddish is recited every day for twelve months."

"No, only eleven."

"Why?"

"You'd better answer that Rabbi Waldbaum."

"The orthodox thinking is that the soul must spend some time purifying itself before it can enter the messianic age to come. For the most evil person, the maximum time required for purification is twelve months."

"Then shouldn't it be said for twelve months, just to make sure?"

"For a mourner to recite Kaddish for twelve months would imply that the parent or relative was an evil person who needed twelve months of purification! To avoid this implication, the Kaddish is recited for only eleven months.

"I know you do not agree, Nathan, but the messianic age has been with us ever since, Yeshua, Adonai's Messiah, began his ministry, was crucified, buried, resurrected and ascended to Heaven's dimensions."

"You are quite right, Jacob. I do not agree. My son, and his mother, my wife, believe as you do. I do not."

"What I recited at the graveside of Steven, today was not a prayer for the dead, but a prayer for the living. Yeshua pointed out in Jerusalem long ago that Adonai is not God of the dead but of the living. Of Abraham, Isaac and Jacob, renamed by Adonai, Israel. All Israel is comprised of those who accept, through faith, Yeshua, as Adonai's Messiah."

"Far be in from me, Rabbi, but I do not believe this Yeshua walked on water."

"Do you know why he walked just that once on water Nathan? Just that once. I will tell you. To show in his genuine humanness, the authority that we humans were supposed to have over the natural world, and lost, because of sin and death."

While Abba and Rabbi Jacob are arguing, Ima is saying to Mary, "Nathan Eigerman, my husband, with a rabbi yet, is showing how stiff is his neck. Apologise to you he should, Mary, for disturbing this day when you have given your Steven a righteous burial."

"I only hope the good Lord finds him righteous."

"Why should He not?"

"I only hope he and his father found faith before they died."

"You loved them dearly."

"Oh, I did. My husband was not perfect but he loved me, and you should have seen Steven when he was a baby."

"Adorable, just like my Stanley."

"Your son is a good boy, I'm glad he's found Jean."

"More than Jean he found. Your grandson yet."

"He calls me his goyish mama. Why Stanley? Shouldn't he have had a Jewish name."

"Nathan, a goyish name, he wanted him to have, so, Stanley. I to him say, 'why Stanley?' and to me he says, 'people will think it a surname,' and call him Mr Stanley."

"Jewish people have a lot to put up with, still."

"Christians too, and Messianic Jews. Stanley, often he speaks to me of Yeshua, then gives me the Messianic Bible to read and now I am one too. You have spoken often to your husband and son Steven about Yeshua, Jesus?"

"A lot. I don't know what good did."

"A good wife and mother you are. A good grandmother you will be. This morning early, I read from the Bible, that the word of Adonai that goes out from the mouths of mothers will not return unfulfilled by Adonai. Such is the love of Adonai, Yeshua, and the *ruach Hakodesh,* the Holy Spirit. Fear, you should not have."

I look around this table, I am content. I am in love with all these people. Ollie and and Paul, talking together. Rabbi Waldbaum and Abba are no longer in conversation, Rabbi and Reverend Williams are discussing the proposal Jean and I put to them. Abba is talking to Steven, and Jean and Hanna, have joined conversation with Ima and Mary.

I experience an intense feeling of joy and well being, I am very happy. *I am glad that You are here to grace this table, Yeshua. Thank You. You are indeed the Lord of the living.*

63

On Tuesday there was a wedding at Kanah in the Galil; and the mother of Yeshua was there. Yeshua too was invited to the wedding, along with his talmidim.

Time passes, I have grown strong working on the farm. I have said goodbye to my last case, closed my office, had my days in court, testifying. Laurence Seymore, Selma and Bradley, and Lucrezia Clemento, tried and found guilty, and it is Tuesday, my wedding day.

The *Chuppa* ~ Canopy has been set up in the field in front of the farmhouse, and the ushers are busy.

I'm a well-dressed Jewish boy, about to be married. I go to Jean. She is in her wedding gown, with her bridesmaids, Mary, Joanna, and Ifeta.

"You're very beautiful."

"My handsome God send."

I take the veil, and place it over her lustrous red hair. I lower the it over her face then lift it.

"I will do this at the ceremony to make sure I'm marrying the right woman, and not being palmed off with Mary here, the way Jacob was with Leah."

"There's worse than Mary."

"Best to be sure." We touch hands.

"Why is my veil so heavy?"

"It was Ima's. Sewn into it are ten coins."

"Why ten coins?"

"My rabbi wants to answer that."

I leave and join my best man.

"Ollie, all set?"

"She lied, Stanley."

"You sure?"

"He was up on the hill. Want to see him?"

We go to the hayshed. There's a man, handcuffed, sitting on a bale of hay, guarded by two of Ollie's men, another has taken charge of a rifle with a telescopic sight.

"Had a clear view from where he was, of your whatyemecallit."

"Chuppa. I'm Stanley Eigerman, and this is Oliver Black, were we your targets?" I say to the man.

"No comment."

"Want to introduce yourself?"

"No comment."

"Who are you working for? Seymore? Or is there someone else?"

"No comment."

"Well, no comment. I'm getting married today, and I'd like you to be my guest. Join in the festivities. It's a joyful day and I'd like you to share our joy and our food and drink."

"Stanley?"

"It's all right, Ollie. Least we can do is to share our meal with him before his time of weeping and gnashing of teeth."

We bring him from the hayshed and walk to the meadow. I call Paul who is head usher and ask him to find a place for my three guests.

"Hallo Artie, didn't know you'd been invited," Paul says.

"What's Arthur's other name?"

"Armstrong."

"Have Arthur and his friends sit on the groom's side, Paul, if you please."
"Keep his bracelets covered."

"Aye, right. No problem."

"Come, Ollie, my betrothal awaits."

With the guests in place, we make our way to a small pavilion behind where they are seated, and in the presence of my father, mother, Joanna, Jean, Steven, Ollie, Mary, and Ifeta, Rabbi Waldbaum and Reverend Williams formally and publically declare us betrothed.

Jean and I drink from the same cup of wine which has been doubly blessed to accept life's joys and responsibilities. Such trembling I never thought would occur, but my right leg takes on a life of its own.

Rabbi Waldbaum blows the Shofar. Two blasts.

He takes the scroll of the scriptures.

Reverend Williams with his Bible stands beside him.

"Blessed is he who comes in the name of Adonai."

They proceed down the centre isle between the seated guests.

The Word of Adonai leads the way in our marriage.

Ollie follows.

Then I, escourted by my Abba and Ima.

The procession of Mary, Joanna, and Ifeta.

Then, Jean, escourted by Steven.

As Steven stands back, Jean comes forward and begins to walk around me seven times. After the seventh, we both move under the *Chuppah*, followed by Ollie and Steven who stand behind us. Jean is to my right. *Daughters of kings are among your favorites; at your right stands the queen in gold from Ofir.*

Rabbi Waldbaum: "Who gives this woman Jean to be married to this man Stanley?"

Steven: "I do." Stepping forward, then back.

Reverend Wlliams: " If anyone here can show just cause why Stanley and Jean should not marry, let him or her speak now or forever hold their peace."

The given time of silence.

Rabbi Waldbaum: "Stanley, Jean, come forward and sign the Covenant of Marriage."

We step forward to the table on which rests the parchment of the Covenant.

I turn to Jean and raise her veil. She smiles at me. Definitely not Leah.

I take the pen, sign my name, and say,

"Be my wife Jean, according to the law of Moses, Israel, and the Messiah Yeshua. I will love, honour, and cherish you as our Messiah loves His holy congregation. I will provide for you as is proper for a husband to do according to the teaching of the Word of Adonai."

Jean signs the Covenant, and says:

"I accept your declaration, Stanley, and dedicate myself to you. I will respect, honour, and cherish you in the same manner as the holy congregation is to love our Messiah Yeshua."

Rabbi Waldbaum, delivers the seven blessings, beginning with:

"Blessed are you, Adonai, the Sovereign of the world who created everything for his glory,"

And ending with: *"Blessed are you, Adonai our God, King of the Universe who creates the fruit of the vine, the symbol of joy. Blessed art Thou, Adonai who has hallowed thy people by the blessing of the marriage canopy, the Chuppah and the sacred covenant of marriage."*

After the seventh, I am handed the cup of wine. Jean and I drink from the same cup, remembering the cup which the will of Adonai gave to Yeshua, and which, for us, he did not refuse.

On the table stands the seven branch menorah. Jean and I light the candles, she from the right, I from the left, to meet at the centre light, the *Shamash*, the servant.

Rabbi Waldbaum: ~

"By lighting the menorah Stanley and Jean are prepared and willing to serve Adonai and one another to keep the fire of their relationship burning. Marriage is like a fire, it goes out if unattended. May their light always shine just as the eternal light shines in the heavenly dimensions."

64

Reverend Williams reads:

Or suppose a woman has ten silver coins and loses one. Won't she light a lamp and sweep the entire house and search carefully until she finds it? And when she finds it, she will call in her friends and neighbors and say, 'Rejoice with me because I have found my lost coin.' In the same way, there is joy in the presence of God's angels when even one sinner repents.

Rabbi Waldbaum begins his address.
"Have you ever wondered about this scripture, and asked yourself why Jesus had chosen a woman, and a lost a coin as an illustration?

"Might He not have said, "When someone (or anyone) loses a piece of silver, don't they light a candle and look for it?

"And, why should the woman call in her friends and neighbours to celebrate over finding the coin? And what does this story have to do with angels rejoicing over a repentant sinner?

"The coin was very important to the woman. In those days, when a man was going to marry he would negotiate a price with the father of the bride. When the price was settled, the young man would give the woman ten coins symbolising a covenant of promise for marriage.

"Meantime, he would return to his father's home to build a house for himself and his bride-to-be. This house, this bridal chamber, would have to meet the approval of the young man's father. When he thought it was good enough, he would tell the son to go and bring his bride.

"The ten coins symbolised the woman's relationship with the bridegroom and so they were very important to her. Every day when the bride would go out she would put on a veil in which she had sewn the ten coins. The veil was an indication to the public that she had been bought with a price, and was waiting to be married. Each coin represented part of the covenant that the man made with the woman. The veil was significant because it separated her from the world and told that she was given to someone for marriage.

"She would wear the veil until the day that the bridegroom came to take her away to the house he had prepared. Sometimes the bride had a long wait because it could take up to a year or more for the groom to build the house to the satisfaction of his father.

"During this time of waiting the bride was consecrated or set apart. She was bought with a price and the ten coins sewn into her veil were evidence of it.

"During that time, she and her bridesmaids would wait with lanterns filled with oil. It was the custom for the groom to come suddenly and since he could come in the middle of the night, the bridesmaids had to have lanterns ready to accompany him.

"If she lost one of the coins, she also lost part of her relationship because the bridegroom may consider her unfaithful or defiled if she didn't have all ten coins when he returned for her.

"In the same way we, who are the bride of Yeshua, Adonai's Messiah, have been given a promise of marriage. It's the new Covenant spoken of by Jeremiah:

"Behold, the days are coming, says the LORD, when I will make a new covenant with the house of Israel and with the house of Judah—not according to the covenant that I made with their fathers in the day that I took them by the hand to lead them out of the land of Egypt, My covenant which they broke, though I was a husband to them, says the LORD. But this is the covenant that I will make with the house of Israel after those days, says the LORD: I will put my law in their minds, and write it on their hearts; and I will be their God, and they shall be my people."

"Yeshua did not pay for his bride with coins. Sin is the Egypt from which Yeshua brought us, forgiving our sins. He has gone to where He is preparing a place for us, and when Adonai decides the time is right, Yeshua will come for his bride.

"So, Stanley and Jean, remain vigilant, faithful to Yeshua, and faithful to each other, so that when our bridegroom returns He will find you faithful, and working to save the souls of sinners for Adonai's Kingdom on earth as it is in the heavenly dimensions. For each repentant sinner Adonai's angels rejoice. Amen."

My Rabbi sits down, Jean's Minister stands up. Before him, we make our vows. Then:

"Do we have a ring for the bride?"

Ollie puts the ring on the proffered Bible. I take it and put it on Jean's finger.

"And with this ring I do thee wed," I say.

"Do we have a ring for the bridegroom?"

Steven puts the ring on the Bible. Jean takes it and puts it on my finger.

"And with this ring I do thee wed."

We both say, "Behold, we are both consecrated one to the other according to the Law of Moses and the Law of Yeshua, the Messiah. Oh, magnify Adonai with us and let us exalt his name together."

I take a glass from the table, smash it at my feet and put my foot on the pieces grinding them, as a reminder of the fragility of life, and a shattering of the past.

Reverend Williams: "Ladies and gentlemen, as witnesses to this covenant of marriage, I now pronounce Stanley and Jean, Mr and Mrs Eigerman. You both may kiss."

From all around us we hear, "Mazel Tov. Mazel Tov."

65

As Jean and I sign the official register, the area, levelled and floored with laminate, where the guests have been sitting is rearranged for our wedding feast.

I say to Ollie, "Will you see that Arthur has a place at the top table, and make sure his hands are free so he can eat and drink."

"Think that's a good idea, Stanley?"

"One of the best, Ollie."

"He'll run."

"Tie his feet together under the table."

"Who's Arthur?" Jean wants to know.

"A man, who did not wish us well. He's been arrested, but Yeshua, wouldn't turn him away at a time like this."

Jean says nothing more but I know she understands.

"Ollie?"

"I'll see to it."

We come from the *Chuppah* and the wedding guests dance around us. Singing, they lift us up, carry us away from each other, then bring us back together again. A quartet of musicians play merry music. Each time we come together we touch hands, before being separated again. Finally we are brought to the high table to be seated.

Before we take our places, I bring Jean to where Arthur is seated beside Ollie.

I smile at him. "Arthur," I say, "This is my wife, Jean. Jean this is Arthur, who is very careless with his soul."

"I'm sorry to hear that, Arthur," Jean says.

"Arthur wanted to make you a widow, Jean."

"Why would you want to do that, Arthur?"

"Why've you got me sittin' here?"

"Because we want you to join us, and eat and drink with us, Arthur."

"Thank you, Arthur," Jean says.

"What for?"

"For not making me a widow. That was a good thing to do."

"Enjoy your meal, Arthur," I say. "I'll come see you in prison. Pour him some wine, Ollie."

Jean and I take our seats, I hear Arthur saying, "He's not all there."

We wine and dine, Abba makes a speech, Steven makes a speech, I make a speech, we cut the cake, the children of our congregations sing: *Dance, dance wherever you may be, I am the Lord of the dance, said He…*

Jean and I sing the metrical version of Psalm 1.

And we dance.

When it comes time for Jean and I to depart, Ollie comes with handcuffed Arthur.

"Artie has somethin' to say."

"Yes, Arthur?"

"Thanks for the dinner."

"I hope you enjoyed it, Arthur," Jean says.

"It was very nice, yes. I'd like to have danced but they tied my ankles together. You said you'd come and see me in prison."

"I did," I say, "and I will."

"They're takin' me away now, so, goodbye."

"God bless you, Arthur. Keep Arthur safe, Ollie."

"I hope you'll be happy."

"Thank you," Jean kisses his cheek. His eye close.

"Stop being careless with your soul, Arthur," I say.

Ollie takes Arthur away.

66

You are to count seven Shabbats of years, seven times seven years, that is, forty-nine years. Then, on the tenth day of the seventh month, on Yom-Kippur, you are to sound a blast on the shofar; you are to sound the shofar all through your land; and you are to consecrate the fiftieth year, proclaiming freedom throughout the land to all its inhabitants.

It's five years now, I'm still married to the same woman, and I'm still a happy man. Steven has a four-year-old step-sister, Esther, who adores him. He is very loving towards her, she follows him around when we visit.

Ollie gave up being Inspector, came into partnership with me, and runs the travel agency Jean and I started when I decided not to be hit on the head any more.

We bought Mr Adgee's farm. His heart failed and he went to live with one of his daughters. I'm part time farmer, part time tour operator, to and from Israel, where Jean and I spent our honeymoon.

At the moment, I'm with Abba in Jerusalem at Hezekiah's Tunnel. Jean, Ima, Jo-Jo, and little Esther are elsewhere in the city. We are here celebrating the Golden Jubilee of Nathan and Esther Eigerman.

"Some tunnel," Abba says.

"It wasn't necessary," I say.

"Marvellous feat of engineering. Of course it was necessary."

"As you say, 'A marvellous feat of engineering', but it wasn't necessary."

"There were the Assyrians, about to lay siege to Jerusalem. Hezekiah knows the city needs water, so he diverts the the upper Gihon river, and builds this tunnel for the water to flow straight down to the City of David. How his engineers managed to make two teams digging from opposite ends meet underground beats me, but I'm told that the teams were directed from above by signals hammered on the solid rock from above."

"The Friends of Zion tell you that?"

"Yes, and I am a friend of Zion. By this achievement Jerusalem's vulnerable point was made strong and what do you call him…"

"Sennacherib."

"Sennacherib, when he saw he was getting nowhere against the walls of Jerusalem, called off his siege. How can you say this water tunnel wasn't necessary?"

"Not me, Isaiah."

"Isaiah?"

"What city did Adonai choose for himself and his people?"

"Jerusalem."

"Did he make a mistake in choosing Jerusalem?"

"Adonai does not make mistakes."

"Did Adonai not know about the lack of a water supply if there was a siege? Was he exposing his people to a deadly risk?"

"He must have known. But there was a risk due to lack of water."

"Suppose yourself in Jerusalem at that time. What would your attitude have been?"

"Same as Hezekiah's. Get a water supply."

"And he did, let me read what Isaiah says,

That day you looked for the armour in the House of the Forest You saw how many breaches there were in the City of David, you collected water from the lower pool, you surveyed the houses in Yerushalayim, tearing some down to fortify the wall. You also built a reservoir between the two walls for the water from the Old Pool; but you didn't look to Him who made these things; you had no respect for Him who fashioned them long ago."

"Adonai, knowingly built his city for his people with a vulnerable water supply so that living in Jerusalem required an attitude and a commitment of faith. What He chose, He would safeguard. Hezekiah abandoned the way of faith, and built himself a tunnel, and he dislocated his relationship with Adonai. It wasn't necessary for him to do that."

"It's still an amazing feat of engineering."

"Of course, it is. We can be as ingenious as we like, but if we do what we do in our own will, and not in the will of Adonai…well."

"Ima wants me to read Isaiah."

"Is Ima pushing it?"

"No, just a suggestion."

"Good. Come, Abba. Let me show you the Pool of Siloam which was where the water of Hezekiah's tunnel flowed to."

67

"Yerushalayim! Yerushalayim! You kill the prophets! You stone those who are sent to you! How often I wanted to gather your children, just as a hen gathers her chickens under her wings, but you refused! Look! God is abandoning your house to you, leaving it desolate." As Yeshua left the Temple and was going away, his talmidim came and called his attention to its buildings. But he answered them, "You see all these? Yes! I tell you, they will be totally destroyed—not a single stone will be left standing!"

Because the incline was steep for Ima to walk all the way, one of our company's people-carriers takes them to the top of the Mount of Olives. Yankl Friedman and Joanna walk behind Ima and Jean, push chairing little Esther. They come from the small church of the Ascension to look over the valley towards the walls of Jerusalem.

Yankl, one of my guides has taken a shine to Joanna who, I think, doesn't mind a bit being shined upon by Yankl.

"Jerusalem in the time of Yeshua wasn't at all like this, Joanna."

"From what Stanley tells me I think I'd rather be here now, than then."

"Unfortunately we still have our troubles. But back then the worst and the best thing happened."

"I know what you're going to say. Stanley's said it too me, so has Ima."

"And I, your Ima, do I not love you, Joanna? That is why I say it to you, Adonai loves us, to Jerusalem he came as Yeshua, He crucified himself because He wants us to be with him without sin."

"Ima, ever since you became a convert to Yeshua you are a fanatic."

"And why can I not be a fanatic? Have I not been commissioned to be? Have not Yankl, and Jean, and Stanley, been commissioned to be Yeshua fanatics? Yeshua, is who commissioned us."

"Your Abba's Judaism failed to be a blessing to all peoples, so God, Himself, provides the blessing. Your abba, my good husband, forever is looking for

Messiah but never sees; forever he hears, but never he understands that his Messiah is Yeshua."

"Ima you become so excited."

"Is not good news exciting? Let your ears hear."

"Why is Grandma shouting?" Esther asks.

"Because she wants Auntie Joanna to hear," Jean says.

"Is Auntie Joanna deaf?"

"Maybe in one ear."

"Will her deaf ear get better?"

"We pray that it will."

"I think Auntie Joanna hears with her good ear."

"Yankl, tell us about the walls of Jerusalem."

"These walls were not here in Yeshua's time, Jean. These are the walls of Suleiman the Magnificent, The walls of Yeshua's time were demolished by the Romans along with the Temple in AD70."

"It was on this hill that Jesus told his disciples that the temple would be destroyed," Jean says. "But He didn't tell them when."

"No, Yeshua didn't tell them when, only that it would take place within the lifetime of that generation of Jews, his generation, which rejected him as Messiah. You see, from the time Yeshua was sacrificed and resurrected, until the time when the temple was destroyed in AD.70, his talmidim, disciples, spread his Gospel to the known world of that time. That was the time known to Adonai."

"You make it sound as if Adonai took revenge on those Jews who killed his son," says Joanna. "Not that I believe Adonai had a son."

"Let us just say that a judgement was passed upon Yeshua's generation and with that judgement an end came to the Old Covenant."

"My father maintains that your Yeshua was a false messiah, just like all the others who perished for their blasphemies, and that the Covenant made with Abraham still holds."

"Do you think Yeshua is Messiah?"

"My father says Yeshua is not the messiah."

"Joanna, my daughter, you love your abba, loyal to him you are, but with your mind you must think, not with his. We move now. Jean, where is Garden of Gesthemene?"

Jean, and the two Esthers walk down the hill leaving Joanne and Yankl together.

"Mother's not pleased with me."

"Won't stop her loving you."

"Nevertheless, I don't want to spoil their time here. She made me think. You see, with Stanley and Ima going the way of Yeshua, I don't want to leave Abba by himself."

"Your mother is still with your father. He is not by himself. Think about what made your mother and brother believe Yeshua is Messiaht."

"What made you believe Yeshua was Messiah?"

"I had to find out what the Prophet Daniel meant in chapter nine verses 26,27. Let's catch up with the others."

"What were those verses?"

"Tell me about them when you read them."

68

Like apples of gold in settings of silver is a word appropriately spoken.

"Welcome back, Stanley."

"Thank you, Ollie, and how are you?"

"No one from our past endeavours, has tried to beam me up into the heavenly dimensions."

"I'll tell you about those dimensions sometime, Ollie."

"It's been five years since we took that rifle from Arthur Armstrong, who by the way, got parole the week after you all went to Israel for Momma and Papa's Golden. I hope you all had a good time together."

"We did. How is Arthur?"

"Fine, came lookin' for you once he got out. Said he see you when you came back."

"You kept an eye on him."

"Didn't want him descending into the lower depths."

"You been readin' Gorky."

"Gorky's good."

"Dostoevsky's better, but not as good as Tolstoy. So where's Artie?"

"Where you arranged for him to be when you visited him in prison. He's on your farm, working with Paul."

"Hoped he'd take me up on that, Ifeta?"

"Ifeta is happy. Good that we thought to introduce her to Mary. With her, she was able to grieve properly for her family. I never thought she'd go with you and Jean to the funeral of the man who murdered them, when that bishop, whatchamacallim…"

"Germanos Kokkinakis."

"Him…buried him. She's living on the farm with Mary, and going to school. Doing well."

"Good to hear."

"How's the missus and my wee God child, Esther?"

"Esther wants to see her uncle Ollie, and so does Jean."

"So, when are we expected?"

"Could Hanna make it tomorrow?"

"Short notice. But sure, we'll be there. Let you know if we can't. By the way, Steve's comin' up in the world."

"Don't tell me. He's taken over the Farmer's Union."

"Not yet. The council elections are on, and Steve's runnin'."

"Which of the parties did he join, or is he going Independent?"

"Unusual Independent."

"How unusual?"

"A Christian Theocrat. Want's to form a political party under that banner."

"I'd say it's more than a banner."

"You're right. He'll have a hard time convincin' people that God's in charge of this world."

"Has he convinced you, Ollie?"

"Boned me a couple of times. Stanley, why have you never boned me about my spiritual state?"

"How long have we known each other?"

"Haven't enough fingers and toes to count the years."

"Boned you every one of those years."

"You never said a word."

"So, how's your spiritual state?"

"I'm a mustard seed man."

"Sooner or later birds will nest."

"Your mother still at your father to read the *B'rit Hadashah?*"

"She's given up on that."

"Leaf out of your book?"

"Worked with you."

"Pappa still think you're more goyish than Jewish?"

"Maintains the suffering servant of Isaiah are the Jews, and not Yeshua."

"Hard nut to crack."

"Might crack from the inside."

"You think so?"

"Up to the *ruach Hakodesh.*"

"Well, as you say, worked with me."

"Knew it would."

"Sister Joanna?"

"Jo-Jo is thinking for herself."

"Having a hard time?"

"She's trying to figure out how to honour her father, if she comes to disagree with him about Yeshua."

"Is that likely?"

"Might be so. She left a suitor back in Israel."

"Ardent?"

"Yankl Friedman, one of my tour operators, He wants a transfer to the Belfast office."

"In pursuit of Joanna, well, well. Goin' to transfer him?"

"Oh yes, he has to explain to Jo-Jo the meaning of Daniel 9:26, 27."

"She needs to know?"

"She does."

"Why don't you tell her."

"She's asked. Best it comes from Yankl. He's on his way here. He'll be working with you."

"What'll you be doin'?"

"I'll be down on the farm with my beloved, and your God child Esther. By the way, if Joanna asks you about those verses in Daniel, don't tell her."

"When I read them, you'll probably have to explain them to me…it was at your wedding…"

"What was?"

"He told me."

"Who told you what?"

"Yeshua, Jesus, Told me He loves me."

"Glad you believe Him."

"Think anybody would publish what we've been through if we wrote about it?"

"They'd say our comedy was so much fiction."

"No foul language."

"No revenge, served cold."

"Too much glorification of *Adonai, Yeshua*."

"No glorification of humans as their own gods."

"Would take the breath of God to save it from rejection."
"Nevertheless…"

Breathe on me breath of God,
Fill me with life anew
That I may love what Thou dost love,
And do what Thou wouldst do.

July heat hits me…

The End.

Ingram Content Group UK Ltd.
Milton Keynes UK
UKHW020638220623
423865UK00007B/378